Lost Seoul

John Mayston

Acknowledgements

I would like to thank David Pickering for his sublime editing skills. He helped bring my story to life and for that I am extremely grateful.

I would also like to thank my wife, Beata, for her support throughout writing this novel. I would have given up if it wasn't for her pestering me to continue. My friends and family have also played a significant part and for that I thank them with my whole heart.

I dedicate this book to our new born daughter, Emily, who was born on 11 May 2015.

Prologue

Is that you? Have you come here to rescue me? Don't leave me here in this hellhole. Please just get me out of here!

'Joe, help me!' I mutter, but there's no response. Then the seriousness of the situation kicks in as my eyes fully open to the surrounding darkness. Suddenly feeling wide awake, I sit up in the bed and come to my senses.

Just another bloody awful dream. And why was I calling Joe's name? I don't need him back in my life…

Moments later I hear a loud, irritable voice outside my door and listen intently. He seems to be grumbling about something.

Still no good. Should've learnt the bloody language.

I hear the familiar sound of jangling keys, so I prepare myself for the worst, but this time he doesn't open the door of my makeshift cell. Instead there's a loud locking sound. The door handle is shaken in frustration and a cold sweat breaks out all over my body as the voice becomes louder and more bad-tempered. Another door is slammed shut and everything turns quiet again.

He always comes in. Why didn't he come in?

Reality dawns.

Was the door left unlocked all night? Was that a chance to escape?

I curl up in a ball on the bed as tears begin to roll down my cheeks.

Just try to get some sleep…

A few hours later, still wide awake, I get up and look out of the tiny window in my room. A glimpse of the sun on the horizon, just starting to rise above the skyline, tells me that it's daybreak. I can just make out the construction workers already working hard in the middle distance as yet another faceless apartment block is slowly raised up from the ground. A plume of smoke from a factory chimney casts its shroud over the buildings, choking the waking inhabitants of this congested city.

It is already very humid and here in my unventilated room my clothes are beginning to stick to my body.

Welcome to another day in hell.

The peace of the night is quickly replaced by the hustle and bustle of working day life. A car stops at the traffic lights and a queue of vehicles builds up behind it, the brake lights glowing red in the thickening smog. As the drivers wait for the lights to change to green, a few of them lose their patience, honking their horns to let off some steam.

If only I could somehow gain someone's attention from down there!

But I'm too high up in this apartment block for anyone to notice little old me up here. Black despair overwhelms me. I can see no hope. No green light ahead of me, just a permanent red one.

Will this suffering never end?

I slump down onto the hard mattress and sob my heart out. As I lie there, I remember the note that I was handed last night. It should be possible now to read it in the morning light. I reach into my bra for it, but then I hear the front door open and slam shut. A shiver runs down my spine so I decide to leave it there a while longer.

He's still seething about something.

I wipe the tears from my face as the key goes in, but it's the wrong one. He tries again.

Is he drunk again?

The door finally opens. He comes in and walks over to me. He hands me a tray and a bag.

'Why no bed clothes?' he demands, towering over me and staring at what I'm wearing.

'I was so tired last night that I fell asleep straightaway,' I say, trying to find an excuse.

3

'Hmm,' he murmurs, clearly unconvinced. 'You wear this tonight.'

He points at the bag. He looks dishevelled and has a five o'clock shadow on his face.

'Eat!' he bellows. Then he leans down towards me and grabs me by the throat. 'Look pretty tonight!' he growls.

He lets me go and straightens up again. His attention is attracted to a framed photo that Rachel gave me of the two of us. It stands on the chest of drawers, having somehow survived the cull of my belongings.

'Just like sexy friend.' He looks at me and I sense he's comparing us. 'I prefer brunette.'

Now I know why he's interested in the picture.

He picks the frame up and touches Rachel's face with a grubby finger. 'She must to come one day.'

I grimace at the thought of my friend being stuck in my predicament.

He catches my expression. 'Why you don't want?' he asks, his brow furrowing.

I can't think why not, you idiot!

He puts the picture back down and looks at his watch, giving the impression that he needs to shoot off somewhere.

'Look good tonight. Mr Lee come.'

I shudder at the thought of that creep being around.

He moves closer, right up to my face. I catch a whiff of stale cigarettes on his clothes and then it hits me.

Oh, God! What's that other smell? That familiar smell of alcohol… what's its name? Soju. Paint stripper, more like! He reeks just like Mr Lee.

I wince.

'He pay good money. He like you. He say you special. He say he want private time. I think you ready, yes?'

I freeze.

'Answer me!' He starts shaking me.

Stay calm.

4

He shakes me harder. Feeling scared to death, I break my silence and tell him what he wants to hear, too scared to oppose him. The shaking stops.

'Good girl.'

He strokes my hair and briefly looks me up and down. *Deep breaths.*

'What this? I never see before.'

I look down to see what he's noticed and shudder as the memories come flooding back to haunt me.

'It's a scar,' I whisper.

He raises his voice. 'Ugly girl no good! Mr Lee pay good money! Cover tonight.'

He looks critically at my face for a few seconds then kisses me on the cheek, right where he slapped me in a fit of rage just a few hours ago. He strokes my hair again and smiles, revealing the gold teeth that I have grown to detest.

'I buy something for face. Last night you make me angry.' He shakes his fist in front of my face. 'Don't anger me again!'

I nod my head while holding in my breath to avoid breathing in his alcoholic fumes.

He gets up, walks to the door and closes it firmly on his way out.

I'm alone again, locked up in my cell. I look inside the bag and see the clothes that he wants me to wear this evening. Yet another short skirt and tight top. My attention turns to what's on the tray.

How I long for cereal and a cup of tea – but just look at this shit I have to eat.

I shovel some of the cold, boiled rice into my mouth. Halfway through eating, and already feeling like I can eat no more, I put the tray on the floor and lie down on the bed.

I scratch another line into the wall with my fingernail and start counting.

If only I could turn back time.

Concluding that he won't be back for a while, I sit up and finally find the courage to reach inside my bra. I find the scrunched-up piece of paper and in a state of breathless anticipation start reading.

Part One
Chapter One

'Come on, Char. Turn that frown upside down. You've been quiet all morning. What's up?'

There is a note of concern in Liz's voice as she busily puts tins of cat food on the shelves.

I stop for a quick breather. 'Well, look at it – just look at it! So much work to do… I don't know about you, but I'm fed up with filling shelves. This job bores me to death.' I look at the mountain of boxes stacked up on the shop floor and then survey the rows and rows of near-empty shelves and feel my heart sink to rock bottom. 'They've given us far too much to get through today.'

'Yeah, I know. They expect us to do more and more every time. I wish I could just get away from it all too, but needs must. I should've studied harder at school but I didn't.' Liz takes off her glasses and cleans them. 'I guess I've accepted this job for what it is. It pays my bills and I suppose I should consider myself fortunate to have one at all.' Her attention switches to me and her face lights up. 'At least you've a chance of progressing, what with your teaching degree. Any idea what you're gonna do with it?'

Her positivity seems to be rubbing off on me as my mood begins to lighten. 'Yeah, I think so. I've been planning an escape route, but I'm a little unsure about what to do next.'

'Sounds interesting. Do tell,' she says, putting her glasses back on and picking up more tins.

I start to explain. 'I saw this advert on the net the other day about teaching English abroad. It's really good money and free accommodation too. Do you think I should give it a try?'

7

'It sounds amazing. Yeah, why not? Give them a call. I know I would.'

'You're right. I get excited just thinking about it.'

She grins at me. 'I can tell. You're positively beaming right now. Compare that to a couple of minutes ago when you looked as miserable as sin.'

'Sorry about that.' I smile at her. 'It could be great, but…'

'But what? Tell me.'

I shrug. 'It's just I worry because my mum says that I can't survive alone and that puts me off a bit. The school's in Seoul and that's a long way away. I don't know, maybe she's right.'

'Oh, don't listen to your mum,' she replies without hesitation. 'She's just worried about losing her little girl. Just do what ya gotta do. I mean, if you're abroad, you're abroad, so it doesn't really matter where you are – and it sure beats stacking shelves, right?'

'Def–' I break off as I glance down the aisle. 'Quick! The boss is coming our way,' I hiss as I grab some tins of cat food.

Our boss marches up to us with a stern look on his face. 'Not much in the way of productivity going on here, ladies. Look at these empty shelves! We don't pay you to stand around chatting all day. Less talking and more–' He stops talking as his mobile phone rings then scurries off to deal with some other problem.

'Bloody miserable git,' she breathes.

I chuckle. 'You always know how to put a smile back on my face. Let's chat about this at break time. Is a quarter past eleven good for you?'

'Yep, sure. Now just you get back to work, Charlotte,' she says, imitating our boss.

'Charlotte?' I echo. It always surprises me when people use my full name, like my mum does. 'Yes, mum,' I respond, sticking my tongue out at her.

We laugh and get back to stacking the endless empty shelves.

I arrive home at four o'clock and sit on the sofa to weigh up calling the agent about the teaching job.

Just give them a call and be done with it!

I finally pluck up the courage, pick up my mobile phone and see that I have been sent a text from Joe.

How r u? Jx.

I think about replying but then decide he's just playing games so I delete his message and tap in the agent's number instead.

'SK Recruitment. How may I help you?' says a woman's voice.

'Hello, can I speak to Mr Bliss, please?'

When the call ends I reflect upon what lies ahead of me.

This is a way out of the tedium I'm living through. A fresh start far away from the ex – and no more stacking shelves!

I decide to have another look through the leaflet that started it all. The excitement bubbles up inside me.

'Yes!' I shout aloud.

They've promised to send me further information. After a couple of sleepless nights, I hear the thud of a parcel hitting the wooden floor at the front door. I hurry downstairs and there's a large package waiting for me. I rip it open and find inside a wire bound booklet with the name of a language school on the front cover. This is what I've been waiting for – the chance of a much more fulfilling life than the one that I've been experiencing all these months!

Flicking through the pages, I'm captivated by pictures of happy, smiling teachers surrounded by children. I'm also drawn to the pictures of tourist attractions to visit in the country.

This looks amazing! I want to be there right now.

I carry the booklet into the kitchen and continue reading it over breakfast. After breakfast, I go back upstairs, sit down on my bed, and carry on flicking through the pages. Eventually I reach the final paragraph.

Free accommodation, flight reimbursed, and four weeks' paid holiday.

It seems an opportunity I cannot afford to miss.

I'm back downstairs again washing the breakfast dishes when my mobile phone rings.

'Hello?'

'Hi, Charlotte. Long time, no see. How are you, darling?'

'Hi, dad. Good to hear from you. I'm well, thanks.'

'So what's been happening in your part of the world, love? Still slaving away at the supermarket?' he asks in a sympathetic tone.

'Yeah. It's pretty dull but I need the money,' I tell him wearily.

'I do worry about you. Are you in debt? You can always come to me for a loan.'

I try to put him at ease. 'No, I'm fine. Honestly, I'm just trying to save a bit.'

'I see. What are you saving for? Spill the beans,' he demands, sounding brighter.

'Oh, it's nothing really. Probably just a pipe dream...' I hesitate for a moment.

'Come on, love. You can tell me anything. You do know that, don't you?'

'I'm just worried about what you and mum are going to think. Promise you'll keep an open mind?'

There's a short silence at the other end. 'I hope it has nothing to do with Joe...' Concern has crept back into his voice again.

'No, dad, he's out of the picture now. It's got nothing to do with him. I haven't seen him for ages.'

Hope I sounded convincing.

'Good. After the way he treated you... If I ever see him again. I'll–'

'Please, no, stop it! Look, what I'm trying to tell you is that I'm...' I pause again.

How can I put it?

'I'm thinking about teaching English abroad,' I suddenly burst out.

'What?'

There's a lull as it sinks in.

'Dad, are you still there?'

'Yes, yes, of course. Well... that's a big surprise – but wonderful news. Where? When?'

I breathe a sigh of relief. 'Judging by the silence, I thought you didn't like my bit of news,' I tell him.

'No, no,' he replies hastily. 'I'll always back your decisions, love. But...' He pauses. 'Your mother might have to be won over though. You know what she's like.'

He says it as if he already knows what she'll have to say about the whole idea.

I tell him that I've been sent a booklet all about teaching in Seoul and that I'm considering applying for the job.

'Why South Korea?' he asks, a little disapprovingly. 'Does it have to be so far away? Why don't you consider somewhere in Europe instead?'

'Dad, you're asking too many questions at the same time. You're confusing me!'

'I'm sorry, love. It's only because I care about you. Okay, I'll shut up and listen.'

So I explain to him about the benefits of going to South Korea. At last he concedes that it would look good on my CV.

'How much will you get paid each month?' he enquires.

'Just over a grand, according to the booklet.'

'That doesn't sound like much to me,' he replies cautiously.

11

'Yeah, but the school provides free accommodation and the taxes are really low,' I point out, trying to reassure him.

'It sounds promising, I have to admit,' he agrees. 'What's the name of the school?'

'Well, the recruiters are called SK Recruitment but I can't remember the name of the school offhand. I'll have a look and let you know. Remind me to do that, otherwise I'll forget – you know what I'm like,' I tell him, trying to keep the conversation light.

He laughs. 'All too well, love, all too well. I'll just jot down that name somewhere. Where's the pad when you need it?' He breaks off for a moment. 'This envelope will have to do. Just one second. Did you say SK Recruitment?'

'Yes, that's right.'

'Okay, done.'

'What do you think mum will say when you tell her?' I ask him nervously. 'She doesn't think I can cope on my own at the best of times.'

'You leave your mother to me. I'm sure she'll be shocked but I'll bring her round to the idea. You know your mother and I will miss you... Seoul's so far away,' he says, with sadness in his voice.

'I know you will. And I'll miss you too. But I'll keep you updated on everything, I promise.' I quickly change the topic. 'Speaking of mum, how is she?'

Later on I opt for a drink at the coffee shop to mull over my plans. There's a lot to consider, so as well as the booklet I take along a jotter pad and pen to scribble down some of my initial thoughts.

I order a cup of coffee and a slice of cake, pay the waitress and locate a free table that's tucked away in a corner of the shop. Once sat down, I flick through the booklet again. Whilst reading, I open up my pad and begin writing a list.

12

First I jot down my concerns. The list seems to go on forever. When it's complete I read through them again – cost of initial flight, travelling alone, language barrier, start-up costs, cuisine, lifestyle changes, making new friends, learning a new language, North Korea. I put down my pen and my mind wanders.

Wasn't there trouble between those two countries some years ago? Perhaps everything is okay now.

I take a bite of cake.

Is this what you really want in life? Oh, pull yourself together! This is what you've been waiting for!

I begin to jot down the reasons why I want to go – adventure, the experience, teaching English, living in a different culture, money, working with children, meeting new people.

Now that sounds much better.

The positives sound so tempting that I want to board a plane bound for the country right away.

Feeling pleased with the exercise, I polish off the last few crumbs of cake and gulp down the rest of the lukewarm coffee. Then I take my phone from my bag to check it for any messages. There's a text from Joe.

I know u still miss me. Why don't we meet up soon? Jx

I start to write a reply, thinking that he really means it this time, but then I remember why I broke up with him in the first place, so I delete both my message and his text.

I try to focus on the reason why I'm here right now. Within a few seconds the clouds disperse in my head and my mood brightens again.

The waitress comes over to my table.

'You look happy,' she says. 'Has something good happened?'

'Yes,' I reply, smiling at her. 'I think I'm going on an adventure.'

Chapter Two

The next day, after a brief conversation with Mr Bliss on the telephone, I call my parents to tell them my latest good news.

'Hi, dad, guess what? I've got an interview!'

'Wow! Congratulations, love. That's great news! When is it?'

'April the thirtieth. Not long to wait now!'

'Whereabouts do you have to go?'

'Oh, it's only in London, so not too far,' I tell him, finding it impossible to keep the excitement out of my voice.

'Make sure you prepare a list of questions,' he tells me in sober tones. 'Remember to ask them about medical insurance and sickness pay. These things are important, love.'

'Yes, I know, dad. I'll sort it.' I try not to sound annoyed with him for not getting as carried away as I am.

'Make sure you do. Any problems, you know where I am. I always have time for you. Your mum is out right now but, of course, I'll let her know your news.'

'Thanks, dad. Thank you for everything.' I take a deep breath. 'By the way, how has she taken it?'

He pauses. 'I'm still working on it, but she's slowly coming around to the idea, I think.'

I thank him once again, and then I end the call without engaging in the usual chatter. I want to get back to scribbling more notes down in my jotter.

In the evening, after a shop-bought ready meal, I get my glad rags on to hit the town with my best friend, Rachel. With her long brown hair, blue eyes and slim figure, she's always one for attracting attention from the boys in town, but I need some time to talk alone with her tonight. The boys will have to be put on hold until we reach the nightclub later on. I need to discuss everything with someone – and she's just the right person for the job.

I have just finished putting on my make-up when I hear the doorbell ring.

'Hi, Char,' says Rachel as I open the door to let her in.

I give her a big hug. 'It's so good to see you!'

She steps back and looks me up and down.

'Wow, you look great! I like the dress. Is it new?'

'Yeah, I bought it the other day.'

'It really suits you. And have you had your hair cut?'

'Yeah. I thought I'd try it shoulder-length. Do you like it?'

She gives my hair a stroke. 'You're a blonde stunner. I won't have a chance tonight!'

We both laugh and we have another hug.

'Aww, thanks, hun,' I tell her. 'You look great too. The taxi's booked in an hour. Shall we crack open a bottle of red first?'

She sighs and rolls her eyes. 'After the week I've had at work, you betcha!'

We sit on the sofa in the lounge with two large glasses of red wine in our hands.

'So what happened at work then?' I ask.

'It's been horrendous. More cutbacks at the office, yet again…which means even more work for those of us who are left–' She stops herself and looks at me. 'I'm so fed up with it, Char. Arseholes, the lot of them! And the wages just don't reflect what's going on in the outside world. It's ridiculous!'

'Yeah, I know what you mean. My salary only just covers the rent and bills.' Then I have a sudden brainwave. 'You could always come away with me, you know?'

'Go away with you where?'

'I'm thinking of teaching English abroad.'

She blinks at me. 'Are you kidding me? Kept that quiet, didn't ya? Why didn't you say anything?'

I can tell that she's a little annoyed with me as well as hugely surprised so I hasten to explain.

'It's not done and dusted yet. You're the first person I've told except mum and dad. I've still got to get through the interview, though I think I'll be fine.'

She shakes her head in bemusement. 'I'm in shock! So where you off to?'

'Seoul. You'll come out to visit me, right?' I say it with sincere hope in my heart.

'If you put me up, I might do.'

'Really? You're not just saying it, are you?'

The thought of Rachel coming out to see me fills me with joy.

'Course I will,' she replies. 'Where exactly is Seoul?'

'Geography never was your strong point,' I joke.

She laughs. 'I was always too busy checking out the lads in class! Mind you, you could be just as bad when you were in the mood for it.'

I pretend to be offended. 'I was as studious as they come, I'll have you know!'

'Erm, not always. You could be distracted just like the rest of us. Remember that time at school when Tom started eyeing you up during an exam? You couldn't resist flirting back. I saw ya!'

'Yeah, yeah, all right. I admit my mind does wander at times, but I can focus when I really have to–'

'I guess you're right,' she concedes. 'You have a degree to prove it. Wish I had one. So go on then, clever clogs, don't keep me in suspense. Tell me where it is.'

'It's in South Korea, next to China.'

'Bloody hell! But that's the other side of the world!' She gives a low whistle. 'That really is quite a distance, babe.' She frowns. 'You know, sometimes you do get these funny ideas in your head. I mean, I think you're clever and that but you do tend to, you know…' Her voice trails off.

'What are you trying to get at?' I say, irritated.

'All I'm saying is in the past you've surprised me at times with some of the things that you've done,' she says.

I have to admit she has some justification for saying it.

'Let's not bring up any of that stuff,' I tell her, still fighting my corner. 'I've grown up a bit now. More mature and more switched on. I've got my degree and I want to make the most of it.'

'I suppose so.' She's still looking serious. 'I hope you're going away for the right reasons though…' She pauses and I have a hunch what's coming next. 'Have you seen scumbag recently?'

'I knew you were going to ask me about him. Nah. Joe's history. He hasn't texted me for weeks now.' The thought of him being *history* triggers something deep inside and seconds later I begin to sob. 'Who am I kidding? He's texted me recently. Rach, I still miss him!'

Her expression becomes tense and I brace myself for the flak that's coming my way.

'How on earth can you bloody miss him?' she snaps at me. 'He was awful to you! I hope you didn't reply to his messages?'

'I thought about it for a while – and I wanted to, really wanted to, but I just couldn't do it. That's why I need to get away from here.' I wipe away the tears that I can feel on my cheeks and then gulp down some wine. 'I'm focusing on the positives – really, I am.' I blow my nose on a tissue and try to sound more upbeat than I feel. 'Look, the money is fantastic and it will pay off so many of my loans. I'm in so much debt…' I pause. 'I really need to get away. Plus, it'll give me some experience of teaching kids. I'm sure it'll look good on my CV when I

17

get back and that will give me an edge over other teachers applying for jobs.' I try to think of any other reasons for going that will impress my friend. 'And I'll be putting distance between me and *him*.'

Rachel's expression softens. 'Finally thinking clearly. I can see your point, babe. Especially wanting to get away from knobhead. Why don't you delete his number?'

'I've really tried but I can't do it just yet,' I tell her. 'I need more time. We were together for ages so it's difficult to forget about him and move on.'

'Okay, but be careful because he's no good for you.' She changes the subject. 'You know that if you do go to Korea I'll miss you, but it's a fantastic opportunity. You're only twenty-one and I can see you wanna go, so just do it!'

That makes me feel a lot better about it all. 'I knew I could count on you for support. And of course I'll miss you too. I hope you'll think about coming out to stay with me.'

'Thanks. I might just take you up on that. If I can save up enough cash, I'll come out to see ya.'

'Great. Fancy a top up?'

'Sure.'

Half an hour later we hear the tooting of the horn from the taxi driver outside. Having just reapplied my make-up, I'm ready to party.

'Right, let's get to the nightclub! There's dancing to be done!'

The queue at the nightclub is long and by the time we get in the place is already packed.

'Looks busy in here tonight,' I shout to Rachel above the music as we work our way through the throng. 'I wonder if we'll see anyone we know?'

'Dunno. Let's have a drink and then pull off some moves on the dance floor!'

After a couple of hours of dancing, Rachel and I decide to take a break and head for the bar. Then I see something that stops me in my tracks. I pull Rachel to one side.

'It's *him*!'

Rachel looks confused. 'Sorry? What ya talking about?'

'Joe! With his mates. Over there.'

She looks where my finger is pointing and spots him just a few feet away from us amidst a group of other people.

'Oh, God. Has he seen you?'

'Not sure. Let's move on.'

But we're too late. 'I think he's spotted you, Char,' Rachel tells me.

'Shit!' I start to panic. 'I don't want to talk to him.'

'It's okay,' she replies, taking my arm in hers. 'I'll do the talking.'

Joe swaggers over towards us.

Even after everything that's happened, I still find him overwhelming.

He comes up close and towers over me. 'Well, well, well, look who's here. Still spreading lies about me?' he demands bitterly.

Rachel places herself between the two of us. 'You don't scare her any more. Just leave us alone, you scumbag!'

We try to get away but he reaches over and grabs me.

'Get off me!' I shout angrily. I try to escape but can't break free from his grasp.

'If you don't get your hands off her, I'll call for security!' Rachel shouts. 'Just fuck off and leave us alone!'

The pushing and shoving gets more aggressive and other clubbers look over to see what the fuss is about.

Joe puts his mouth to my ear. 'It ain't nice being ignored.' His anger goes up another notch as he pulls

19

away and glares menacingly at me. 'This ain't over, bitch!' Then he finally lets go of me.

Two bouncers who have noticed the commotion come over as Joe returns to his mates. He looks back and points his finger at me before turning away.

'Are you two all right?' asks one of the men.

'Yes, we're fine now, thank you,' says Rachel.

The bouncers nod and drift off.

Rachel hugs me and I sob uncontrollably for some time. She suggests that we should make our way over to the toilets, where it is a bit quieter so that we can talk properly. Once there, I look in the mirror over the sink and see that I look a mess, with mascara running down my face.

'I still love him,' I say in a pathetic voice.

'You've drunk too much,' she decides. 'You mustn't go near him again, okay? Do you remember what he did to ya? He–'

'I know!' I interrupt. 'Stop fucking reminding me! But he's still got this stupid, crazy hold over me. What on earth am I gonna do, Rach?'

She puts her arm around me and looks concerned. 'I do worry about you, babe. Look at me. Are you sure you're in the right frame of mind to go abroad?'

'I have to go. I want to go. I want to get away from here, from *him*. A fresh start… Come with me, please? I'm begging you. You could get away from your ex too!'

'You can't compare our ex-boyfriends. Yours was a monster compared to mine and the sooner you see that the better!' She sighs. 'I'm sorry, but living abroad – well, it's just not my bag, babe.' She purses her lips apologetically. 'Come on. Let's try to enjoy the rest of tonight. Shall we get back on that dance floor?'

'Can we go home? I'm really gutted because he's ruined our night. I was really looking forward to it.'

She strokes my hair. 'All right, babe. Let's get you home to bed.'

She takes my hand and guides me out through the busy nightclub. I scan the dance floor for Joe.

'You're all right now, hun,' Rachel comforts me. 'I'll look after you.'

The next morning I spend mostly in bed with an all too familiar hung-over feeling. Eventually I find some energy and drag myself out from under my duvet, put on my dressing gown and slippers and slowly shuffle my way over to the bathroom. I look in the mirror and see mascara still smudged all over my face.

You look a right state. No more alcohol for you for a long time, young lady.

I open the bathroom cabinet and search for some aspirin. The dull ache inside my head makes me want to go back to bed but I have things to sort out.

I check my phone but there are no new messages so I send Rachel one.

Hi, hun. So sorry about last night. Head hurts! x

I hear my phone beep some ten minutes later so look at the screen and see that Rachel has sent me a reply.

I've a sore head 2. Please stay away from him. Hope ur ok? x

I think to myself how fortunate I am to have such a good friend before wearily setting about my mundane tasks.

Chapter Three

'Mr Bliss is ready to see you now,' says his secretary.

This is it.

I get up from the chair and am led through for the all-important interview. Mr Bliss is sitting at his desk and welcomes me into his office with a pleasant smile.

He's quite different to how I imagined him to be when I spoke to him on the telephone. I see before me a middle-aged man with small, brown eyes, receding hair, and a round, chubby face. I imagined him to be younger so this takes me somewhat by surprise but I think I manage to conceal it.

'It's so nice to meet you. Please call me Colin. Would you like tea or coffee?'

'A glass of water would be perfect.'

He looks at me intently. 'So have you had a good look through our booklet?'

He smiles as he says it and I'm already beginning to feel comfortable in these friendly surroundings.

'Oh, yes. It all looks amazing! It makes me want to be there right now.'

'Well, that's what I like to hear,' he says, rubbing his hands together. 'You know, looking at you I have a feeling that this is going to work out just fine. If you get the job, I feel sure that you will prove to be an asset to the school.'

The interview lasts the best part of an hour as Colin asks me various questions about my qualifications and why I want to teach English abroad. His salesman's voice at least sounds the same as it did on the telephone. It's the type of voice that could sell ice to the Eskimos. Towards the end of the interview the conversation turns to finances.

'Did you read the section on paying money up front?' he asks.

'Erm, no,' I admit. 'I didn't. Can you please explain everything?'

Why do I never read things properly?

'The booklet clearly stated everything but anyway, not to worry, certain things need to be paid for in advance. The flight tickets have to be bought by you. The first month will be financially difficult but this is where we can help you out. We can offer you a loan of up to two thousand pounds to help pay for your flight tickets and set up your apartment in Seoul.' The expression in his eyes expresses both an apology and a reassurance and I know I can trust him.

Flicking through the contract pages, he draws my attention to the cost of the flight ticket being reimbursed three months into the contract.

'We'll deduct the money in small, monthly instalments from your salary so you won't feel the pinch too much. Now, I can see you need time to think about this but it's all written in the contract.'

He hands me a copy of the contract which amounts to twenty-five pages.

'There's a bonus scheme for you to look at on page twenty-three,' he points out.

'A bonus scheme? That sounds very interesting. I'll take a look at that for sure,' I say, feeling slightly happier about the financial side of the deal.

I leaf through the document to page twenty-three and am taken in by the pound signs.

My student loans will be paid off in no time!

'I'm sure you must have some questions you'd like to ask me,' he says.

So I reel off my list of questions. He says there are some things that he'll check up on and get back to me as soon as possible. Despite this, I'm very impressed with the set up of his company.

'We'll be in touch shortly' he continues. 'I'll get the contractual details sorted out within the next week or so, if I decide that you're a suitable applicant. I'll need to take some personal details and I'll also need a passport-sized photograph too.'

I nod my head and consider what he's just told me.

Of course he needs more information. There will be work visas and things he will have to organise.

'Is that okay?' he enquires, trying to guess what I'm thinking.

'Yes, that's fine. I'll look through everything as soon as possible and get that photo ready for you.'

'Oh, one more thing. Can you sing?'

For a moment I'm flummoxed. 'Well, yes, I can. In fact I won a singing competition when I was at school,' I add, trying to impress him.

He smiles. 'Oh, that's perfect.'

'Why do you ask?'

'There's lots of singing to be done with the younger ones so you have to be prepared to lead the occasional sing-along. I hope you know your nursery rhymes,' he chortles.

'Oh yes, I do. I love a good sing-along. It all sounds wonderful!'

We say our goodbyes and I leave the office feeling pretty confident that I will be offered a position in the coming week. As I walk towards the underground station, I run through the main points of the interview in my head.

Free accommodation, bonus scheme, flight ticket reimbursed, picked up at the airport… Seems all right to me – but I must make sure I read through everything.

Two hours later I arrive back home at my flat, slump down on the sofa and drift off to sleep, only to be awoken by my mobile phone ringing some twenty minutes later.

'Hi love, how did you get on?' asks mum.

'Hi, mum.' I pull the phone away from my ear and yawn. 'Sorry, you've just caught me having forty winks. I'm totally exhausted.'

'I thought you'd be tired. So go on then, tell me what happened.'

I brace myself for the interrogation.

'Well, I have to wait a few days but I think they're going to offer me the job. I've already been given a contract to look at.'

There's a long pause as my mother takes it in. 'Such a big step. Please read through it carefully, love. Why not get your dad to look at it? You know how you tend to skip over things.'

'I don't skip over things! I'll make sure I look through it thoroughly as soon as I get the chance.'

'Well, just make sure you do. You remember your trip to the hospital in Ibiza when you…'

I cut her off in mid-sentence. 'Mother, can you stop bringing that up, please? It was a stupid mistake. I thought I had insurance cover for two weeks.'

'Just the one week, though, wasn't it? And it was all because you failed to look through the paperwork. You broke your arm, love, and who had to foot the bill?'

She's never going to let me forget that…

'I was seventeen,' I tell her wearily. 'I've grown up a lot since then.'

'Well, sometimes I wonder. You always seem to be failing to pick up on things or having some kind of misunderstanding over something or other. And as for your choice in men – well!'

'Please, mum, don't bring him into this.'

This is how it always goes – my mother managing to get me het up over my failings.

She's just getting into her stride now. 'It was obvious to everyone that it would end the way it did, but you just turned a blind eye to it all.'

25

'I can't believe you're raking over this yet again,' I tell her, trying not to lose my temper. 'I promise I'll look through the contract with a fine tooth comb, okay?' I pause for a moment as I don't want us to have a row over this. 'I want to make you both proud of me, so can't you just be happy for once?'

There's a short silence at the other end of the line.

'I'm sorry, love. Perhaps I'm being a little over-critical,' she admits.

'A little?'

'Look, Charlotte. Of course we're proud of you – after all, you're our only daughter and we love you dearly. I'm only looking out for you and saying these things because I care about you. South Korea is so far away and of course we're going to miss you if you do go. I'm not sure whether I want you to go but your father thinks it might be good for you. Just think about things clearly, okay?'

I try to remain positive. 'I'm twenty-one now and you have to let go, mum. I really want to do this.'

She softens her stance a little. 'Why don't you come over and see us and let your father look through your contract for you? It'd be good to have a second pair of eyes run through everything.'

'Yes, it'd be good to see you both,' I concede.

'And the contract?' she enquires.

'Okay, I'll bring that with me too.'

So we arrange to meet up the following weekend. After the call ends, I give a long groan and sink back onto the sofa.

Chapter Four

It's six o'clock in the morning and I require a nice strong cup of coffee to wake me up a bit. I put the teaching contract down on the table and read the first few pages as I eat my breakfast. I still haven't found the time to read it in full but I know I can leave the details to dad when he looks at it later on in the day.

While I'm washing up the breakfast plates, the phone rings. It's mum again.

'Hi, love, just checking that you're up and ready,' she tells me, as though I'm eleven.

God, can't she have some faith in me for once?

'Mother, you don't have to check up on me. I'm not a little girl any more,' I say, only half-jokingly.

'Well, this is a great start to the weekend and you haven't even arrived yet!' she replies, sounding annoyed.

'Sorry, I was only messing around. Couldn't you tell?'

'Oh, I see. I'm never sure with you. Let's just forget about it, okay?' she says wearily.

'Okay, mum. I'm looking forward to seeing you both. Dad's meeting me at the station, right?'

'Yep.' Her staccato response gives me the impression all is still not well. She pauses for a moment and I can sense she is trying to gather her thoughts. 'There was something else I was going to ask you but I've forgotten what it was, what with our little spat.'

'I'm sure it will come back to you later. Anyway, I must get on now so I'll see you in a bit.'

'Okay. See you later,' she says as she hangs up.

I finish off washing the dishes and go to my room to pack my bag. As I'm packing, I hear my phone beep in my pocket so I take it out and see that I have received a text message from Rachel.

Know u r off 2 ur parents but please call me. Rx

What's troubling her?

I finish packing and, once ready, leave my place and walk down the street towards the railway station. I call Rachel along the way.

'Hiya. Just read your text. What's up?'

'I saw my ex last night,' she blurts out. 'He was with another woman and he was holding hands with her. In public! I mean, how could he? The bastard! We only broke up three fucking weeks ago!'

She sounds distraught.

'I'm sorry to hear that, Rach. I know you're angry but you need to rise above it.' I pause to collect my thoughts. 'You know what I think about him. You can do much better.'

I can sense that it hasn't gone down well.

'What – like your ex?' I sense she wants to take back her words as soon as she has said them. 'Oh, I'm sorry. I didn't mean that. Just caught up in the moment.'

There's a lengthy pause. Neither of us knows what to say next. I'm the first to break the silence.

'I really wish I was with you now to give you a big hug. As soon as I'm back in town, I promise I'll come over to see you. Why don't you make yourself a cuppa and go back to bed? It's still early.'

'I couldn't sleep last night, which is why I'm up so early – but I don't really wanna go out today. I think I'll just lounge around the house,' she says, sounding fed up.

'I promise to visit soon, hun, but I'm on my way to the station and there's a lot of background noise. I'll text you on the train. Are you sure you're going to be okay?'

Rachel sounds a bit calmer now. 'Thanks, hun. I don't know what I'll do without you if you get this job in Seoul.'

'I tell you what. We certainly know how to pick bad apples, hey? Me and you are besties and I'll always be there for you. Take care and I'll text you in a bit.'

'Okay. Thanks. Chat soon.'

It's only a short wait until my train arrives at Hemel Hempstead station. I get on, find a spare seat and send Rachel a text to try to cheer her up. While I wait for a reply, I look out of the window and see the beautiful green rolling countryside that's passing me by. It makes me think how much I'm going to miss it when I leave the country.

Hours pass by before I finally get off the train at York and see dad waiting for me on the platform.

'Hi, love. Come here. It's so good to see you,' he says, embracing me as though I'm still his little girl.

'Hi, dad. It's good to see you too. We've so much to catch up on. It's been a while.'

'Come on then, let's get you back home so you can see your mother.'

The journey home is an enjoyable one and gives me a chance to catch up with what's going on in my parents' lives. Thirty minutes later, we pull up at the house and dad gets my bag out of the boot.

'I'll just put this in your bedroom,' he says.

I go into the kitchen, where mum is making herself busy and move towards her cautiously, our morning conversation still fresh in my mind. She's wearing a flowery dress and looks absolutely stunning, which makes me realise why my dad married her, despite her shortcomings.

I kiss her on the cheek. 'Hi, mum.'

'Hello, Charlotte.' Her manner is rather cold and I sense she's waiting for an apology so I hold out an olive branch.

'Can we forget about this morning? I was only playing around and I just want us to have a nice weekend together. Can we, please?' I beg.

'I only say these things because I care about you. I just want you to be happy,' she replies.

'I know you do and I am. Really, I am! I've never been so pumped up about anything in my life before. I want to make both of you proud of me – you know, stand up on my own two feet. It's a great opportunity.'

'I can tell you want to go to Korea, love. I'm still not sure, but let's just get your dad to read through the–'

The contract! You idiot! You left it on the bloody kitchen table!

'Is everything okay?' she asks, seeing my expression.

How am I going to explain this one?

'Mum, please don't kill me, but I was distracted this morning because Rachel sent me a text. I…' I falter as I anticipate her reaction.

'Spit it out, love.'

'I left the contract on the kitchen table.'

Mum just stares at me. 'Oh, well done, Charlotte. Well done. And you think you'll be able to look after yourself on your own out in Korea!' She emits a bark of bitter laughter.

'I'm sorry,' I say, just managing to get my words out before bursting into tears.

'I mean, Korea for God's sake! All those nuclear missiles sent flying around by Kim Jong what's-his-face's regime in North Korea – even for you this is quite ridiculous! I've tried to see it from your point of view but the fact is I think it's a perfectly terrible idea!'

I'm sobbing uncontrollably now. I hear dad hurrying downstairs to see what the matter is.

'What on earth's going on? You two have only been with each other for a couple of minutes and you're already having a barney! Can't we just have a nice, relaxing weekend?'

Mum glares at him. 'She's only gone and forgotten the contract, Peter. What are we going to do with her and these crazy notions that she has?' She sniffs loudly. 'She gets that from you, you know. Going to Korea… Pff!'

'I thought you were mellowing to the idea?' Dad tells her. 'Can't you be a bit more supportive? Look at our daughter right now. Look at what you're doing to her.'

30

Mum throws her arms up in the air and then turns away to start preparing lunch. She's clearly decided to withdraw herself from the whole business.

Dad puts his arm around me and tries to calm me down. Once I'm feeling composed again, he addresses the problem under discussion.

'Did the recruiter send you an electronic copy?'

'No, only a print version. I'm really sorry, dad. I got distracted this morning. First mum called, then Rachel sent me a text. I was actually reading it at breakfast as well!' I add, feeling really annoyed with myself.

'When are you expecting the recruiter– what's his name?'

'Colin.'

'When are you expecting him to make a decision?'

'Some time next week.'

'Right. Well, you must read it thoroughly. Now let's enjoy our weekend together. We've planned some nice little surprises for you. Truce?' he says, looking at both mum and me.

'Okay,' I reply. 'Truce. You're right. Let's make the most of our time together.'

I go over to my mum and give her a hug. We agree to put our differences to one side for the weekend and try to enjoy each other's company.

Chapter Five

I'm awoken by the ringing tone on my mobile phone. Unwilling to get up just yet, I blindly reach my hand out to the bedside table and try to locate it.

'Hello? Is that Charlotte?'

Who on earth is it?

'Speaking,' I say, still confused as to who I'm actually talking to.

'Hi, it's Colin from SK Recruitment. How are you?'

I try to wake myself up. 'I'm a bit tired but I'm fine, thank you.'

'I'll get straight to the point. I'm delighted to inform you that you've been a successful applicant. We'd like to offer you a position at the Sinchon language school in Seoul, starting next month. Now, I understand that you may need some time to think about this but I'd also like to add that I don't want you to mull over things for too long as the position needs to be filled relatively quickly. What do you think about my proposal?'

I pause, my heart's beating rapidly.

'Charlotte, are you still there?' he asks.

'Yes, yes,' I splutter. 'This… This is great news! I'm just trying to take it all in…'

'Perhaps you'd like me to call back in half an hour or so. Iron out some details?' he suggests.

'No, no. It's fine. I really want the job.' I'm trying hard to keep the extent of my excitement out of my voice.

'That's excellent news,' he tells me. 'I recall giving you a copy of the contract. Do you still have it?'

'Yes, I have it to hand,' I say, trying to remember exactly where I've put it.

'All you need to do is sign and date it and pop it in the post along with a photocopy of your passport details and a letter of job acceptance so we can start the process of your visa application. Oh, we also need a photo of you too.'

'Okay, I'll look through it before I go to work and get all of it in the post as soon as possible.'

'Good. Do you have any other questions?'

I can't think of a thing to ask him. In fact I can't think at all. 'Not at the moment.'

'I'll be in contact soon. Have a lovely day – and well done.'

The call ends and I jump up in the air shouting 'Yes!' as the adrenalin kicks in. I ring my parents to tell them the good news, but there's no answer. Then I remember that dad mentioned they were going away on a hill walking holiday in Scotland. I try his mobile but there's no reception up in the Cairngorms so I'm unable to leave a message.

You're a big girl now. They can only do so much for you. It's time you made your own decisions.

My mobile rings. I answer it and recognise the voice of my supermarket manager.

'Hi, Charlotte. John's called in sick. Can you come in a bit earlier and do some overtime for me?'

Bloody hell! Not again.

But I need all the money that I can get, so I confirm that I can do it and get into my work uniform. I'm smiling, however, as I set off to work. It'll take more than that to depress me after the news from Colin.

The following day I get another early morning call from the recruitment agency.

'Hi, Charlotte – it's Colin. Have you looked through the contract details yet?'

I become very wide awake. 'Hi, Colin – sorry, I was busy with work all day yesterday as I was asked to cover for someone. I was going to look at it today.'

'Do you think it would be possible for you to pop it in the post today? I'm sorry to press you but we really need to get the ball rolling.'

'I totally understand. I'll do it right away,' I promise.

'Excellent. I'll call the school in Seoul to confirm your acceptance once I have received your contract.'

The call over, I make myself a cup of tea and set about reading the contract. Then my mobile rings again.

'Hi, Charlotte,' says my supermarket boss. 'John's called in sick again. Can you cover his shift? It starts at twelve which gives you just over an hour to get here. We are really short-staffed today and desperately need your help.' He sounds like he's on the edge of panic.

'I'd love to but–'

'Wonderful – see you in an hour. Thanks once again. You're a star. Must go now.' And he rings off.

Well, that's just great. That man's such a git! I'm going to have to bloody race through reading the contract now!

I rush to my bedroom and hurriedly get showered and dressed into my work clothes, then go back downstairs and brew another cup of tea. I sit down and try to address myself to the contract, but time is against me and end up just skimming through it.

You have to get to work! Just sign it and get out of here.

So I sign it and find a stamp and an envelope to put the contract in. As I leave for work I can hear my mother's voice ringing in my ears. *What on earth are you playing at?*

I post the contract in a letterbox.

That's that. Job done.

A few days later the start date is finalised by Colin. I'm due to begin teaching in just under a month's time, on the ninth of June.

Chapter Six

As the departure date draws ever closer, I begin to panic about getting everything done on time. I book the flight and am due to arrive in Seoul on the seventh of June. My parents have agreed to take me to Heathrow Airport to see me off, which is good of them. I still have a lot of essentials to buy, but at least my leaving party at an Italian restaurant in town is all arranged.

The evening comes around surprisingly quickly.

'Awesome choice of restaurant,' says Rachel as she gives me a hug and hands me a card and present, along with a good luck balloon. 'Where's everyone else?'

'Aww, thanks for the gift. I'll open it later. You're the first to arrive but I'm expecting five other people. Wow,' I observe, looking her up and down, 'you look stunning.'

'You look fabulous too. Do I know any of the others coming?'

'I think you've met Paul, Steven and Liz from where I work.'

'Oh, yeah. That time we went to the pub together and did the quiz.'

'That's right. I don't think you know the others but I'll introduce you to them later on.'

My other friends arrive shortly after and each of them hand me a card and present. Halfway through the meal, however, my enjoyable evening is turned on its head.

'Shit!' Rachel whispers in my ear. 'I think twat-face has just walked in with a few of his mates.'

'What? Oh, for Christ's sake – that's all I need!'

'Look, just relax,' Rachel mutters. 'He can't do anything to you here, can he? It's a big restaurant and he might not even see us.'

'I suppose not. It's just bloody typical of him to turn up!'

A few minutes later Joe heads for the toilets, which happen to be next to our table. With a sinking heart I realise he has spotted me and is coming towards us.

'What's going on here then?' he demands as he reads the message on the balloon. 'Good luck, Charlotte. So go on then,' he continues with a smirk, 'tell me your news.'

'She doesn't have to tell you anything. Why don't you sod off back to your mates!' shrills Rachel.

Joe looks down at her. 'Always speaking up for her, aren't you? You need a new hobby, darling.' He turns back to me. 'Can we just talk in private, away from this emotional nutter?'

I glance at Rachel and it looks like she's going to blow her top but Liz puts an arm around her and manages to calm her down a little.

'We're just trying to have a nice evening,' I tell him. 'I don't think there's anything we have to say to each other.' I can feel my face beginning to burn up.

'Just five minutes,' he insists.

'Don't go – you'll regret it,' Rachel warns me.

I sigh. This is all getting so embarrassing. 'I'll just be five minutes,' I tell Rachel as I rise from my chair. 'I'll be all right. Don't worry about me.'

Rachel looks utterly pissed off with me. 'Fine! Just don't come running back to me when it all goes wrong.'

I leave the table and Joe leads me out of the restaurant. It's a warm evening and I catch a glimpse of the sunset between the buildings around us. Joe doesn't waste any time getting down to business.

'So what's going on then? What's with the good luck balloon? Do you have a new job or something?'

There's a boxing match starting inside my head. I'm trying to decide how much to tell him. I decide to tell the truth.

'I'm going away...' I struggle to get it out. 'Not that it concerns you.'

'Oh. Right. Where to?'

36

'I'm going abroad. Teaching English, if you must know.'

He stares at me, then laughs. 'You're going abroad? And how are you gonna survive? All by yourself, all alone. How much did I have to do for you when we went out together?'

'I can do things for myself,' I retort, while wishing I was sounding less unsure.

'Fuck off!' he sneers. 'You know you still need me. Remember that time I was there for you in your hour of need? You would have died if it hadn't been for me saving you. You can't have forgotten that, can you?'

'Stop it! Just stop it!' I yell at him. Tears start to fill my eyes as I recall what happened.

'See? Admit it – you need me!'

I try to defend myself from his taunts. 'You may have been there for me then but what about all the other times? The pain you put me through! I might not have been able to stand up for myself then but I've…' I search for the right words but can't find them.

'You've what? Progressed? I don't think so, darling.' He shakes his head. 'Why are you talking to me now? If I've put you through hell, like you say, why are you still willing to talk to me?'

I feel he's twisting everything, like he always does. 'Please, don't do this to me. I still–'

'You still what? Love me?'

I begin to sob. 'You're such a tosser!' I shout through my tears. 'I hate the way I feel about you!'

At that moment, Rachel opens the door and rushes out to where Joe and I are standing. She hears me crying and that pushes her button. She goes up face to face with him.

'Just fuck off! You treated her like shit. She's going away and she ain't coming back for a long time!'

I slump to the ground in a heap, barely able to comprehend what is going on around me. Joe grabs Rachel and starts shaking her violently from side-to-side.

'You bitch! You're always interfering in my business. Why don't you just do us all a favour and fuck off yourself!' he snarls at her.

'Stop it, Joe!' I protest feebly.

I look up and can just make out another figure emerging from the restaurant. Through my tears it looks like a man in a uniform. Then I see it's the waiter who's coming to our rescue.

'Hey! If you don't leave here now, I'll call the police,' the waiter shouts at Joe.

'Who the fuck do you think you're talking to, penguin boy?' Joe shouts back. 'Want some of my fist in your face, do ya?'

Joe grabs the waiter and starts to plough his fist into his body. The waiter tries to fend him off but Joe overpowers him and he is soon laid on the floor, rolling around in agony. I see Rachel edge closer to the restaurant door as she tries to escape from Joe but he spots her and grabs her waist, dragging her back over towards me kicking and screaming. He pushes her to the ground next to me.

'You fucking bitches! I've had it with both–'

He stops in his tracks as he spots his mates fleeing the restaurant.

'Oi, Joe!' one of them shouts. 'Get the fuck out of here! The manager's called the pigs!'

Joe leans down close to my face and I can feel his breath on my skin. 'This ain't finished. Believe you me!'

Rachel gets up. 'She's going and there ain't a damn thing you can do about it! Oh, is that police sirens I can hear? Just fuck off!' she screams with every last ounce of her energy.

And with that Joe runs away down the street and the last I see is him heading off into the woods at the end of the road.

'Geez!' Rachel breathes. 'You okay, Char?'

I'm still shaking and unable to move. The manager of the restaurant comes out and helps the waiter back onto his feet, taking him back inside. Steven and Paul come outside to find us.

'Where the hell were you two?' Rachel snaps at them. 'Thanks for helping us out. Surely you could see that we were gone for a long time! Didn't you hear anything?'

They look apologetic. 'We're very sorry. We honestly couldn't hear anything,' says Paul.

By now, all I want to do is get home and go to bed. Reading my mind, Rachel pipes up.

'I'll book a taxi and take you home,' she says. 'Seriously, steer clear of that wanker from now on. You've seen what he's capable of. Just forget about him.'

She gets her phone out and calls for a taxi, then gets me back onto my feet and slowly walks me back inside the restaurant, where she sits me on a chair at the bar. 'Wait here and I'll settle up with the others.'

Fortunately, the taxi arrives in no time at all and I stand up gingerly to say goodbye to my friends.

'Are you okay now?' asks Liz, who looks really concerned.

'Yeah, I'll be fine. Rachel's here to look after me now.'

'I shall miss you so much at work, Char,' she says. I can tell she really means it.

'It's a terrible job,' I reply, welling up inside, 'but you brightened up my day for sure. I'll definitely miss you too.'

We walk outside together and Rachel insists that she gets in the taxi with me as she wants to see me home

39

safely. Ten minutes later we arrive back at my place. She pays the fare and walks me to my front door.

'Do you want me to stay with you?' she asks.

'I'll be fine. I just want my bed.'

'I can sleep on the sofa. I just wanna make sure you're okay.'

'I'll be fine. I'm home now, safe and sound.'

She takes a deep breath. 'So this is it then. The last time…' She can't continue.

'Yes, this is it – but we'll keep in touch. God, I'm going to miss you!'

We share an embrace.

'I know you're doing the right thing,' she says, pulling away at last. 'You need to get away from here for a while.' She fishes around for something in her bag. 'I've got you this. It's not much but it may bring back happy memories. Please take it.'

Rachel hands me a framed photo of us when we went away on holiday some years ago.

'Oh, it's beautiful. Thank you so much.' I kiss her on the cheek. 'I'll definitely take it with me. It'll remind me of the good times. And I'll read the guidebook you gave me as well.'

'Yeah, it's got some info on good places to visit.' She gives me a serious look. 'Are you sure you're gonna be okay?'

'Yes. I'll call you once I've settled down in Seoul,' I reassure her.

With that she sets off down the road. I shut the front door and look down at the photo she's given me.

I miss you already.

Chapter Seven

The day has finally arrived. Shortly I'll be on the plane to South Korea. I feel really excited but at the same time a little anxious about what lies ahead of me. I pack all my things, including the picture that Rachel gave me, and clean the entire rented apartment from top to bottom. A few hours later, at around midday, my parents arrive and help me put my luggage in the car. The things I don't need will go back to their house. Just before I leave, I hand the keys back to my landlord and then we are on our way to Heathrow.

'Now, have you got your passport?' asks mum.

'Yes, mum,' I reply, rolling my eyes.

'Well, we don't want to have to do any U-turns, do we?' she says in that all-too-familiar tone of hers.

'I do know how to pack, mother!' I exclaim in exasperation.

'Come on, you two,' dad interrupts. 'For goodness sake, stop bickering. We've only just got in the car!'

I do my best to cope with mum's comments as it's our final day together for a long time. About an hour later we park the car at the airport and dad carries my bags to the check-in desk.

The queue for check-in is quite long. I catch a glimpse of mum and sense that she is itching to get something off her chest.

'So what is happening at the other end? Is someone going to meet you at the airport?' she says, deciding to test my knowledge on airport arrangements in South Korea.

'Colin e-mailed me to say that a representative from his company will meet me there.'

'Oh, that's good. And do you know that person's name?' mum asks.

'Yeah, I've written it down somewhere on a piece of paper.'

She tuts. 'Somewhere? Make sure you don't lose it then. You know what you're like. Like father like daughter.'

'Don't bring me into this,' says my father grumpily.

'Geez,' I tell her. 'Would you just give me a break! I'm sure I put it in my bag this morning.'

'Are you sure you're sure?' enquires mum, only half joking.

'Yes, of course I am!'

'Sorry, love. I only say these things because I care about you.'

Once I have checked in, I walk over to the departure gates with my parents in tow.

'Oh, I've forgotten something,' says mum suddenly.

'You mean to say your memory isn't perfect?' I mutter.

'I'll pretend I didn't hear that. I'm just popping to the shop to buy you some mints. It's always good to have them on hand during a flight.'

She wanders off.

Dad takes my arm. 'Now your mum's out of earshot, I wanted to check if you read the contract in detail like you said you would.'

'Yep. I looked at it before I went to work a good few weeks ago,' I tell him.

'Good. And did everything seem all right to you?'

Feeling uneasy, I try to nip the conversation in the bud.

'Yeah, it all seemed fine to me.'

'Really? Are you sure? You sound unsure.' He looks at me with concern etched on his face.

I don't want him to worry about me so I tell him a white lie. 'I have a friend who specialises in contract law. We went through it together with a fine tooth comb.'

I'm going to hell! But it's in a good cause. I hope he buys it.

'That's great. Your mother will be pleased to hear that and I know that I am too.' He gives me a hug. 'You know, I'm going to miss you so much. Your mother too, underneath that tough exterior of hers.'

'I'm going to miss the both of you too. You mean so much to me but we both know I have to do this because I'll learn so much from this experience, won't I?'

'Yes, you will, darling. I wish you all the luck in the world.' He digs in his pocket and pulls out an envelope. 'Here's some currency to get you started.'

I'm somewhat taken aback but before I can say anything mum bears down on us once more so I stuff the envelope away and give him another hug.

'Here are the mints,' says mum. 'Can I have a hug too, or is this just a father–daughter thing?'

'Of course, mum. Come here.' I give her a tight hug. 'I won't let you down. I want to prove to you that I can do this.'

'I know, love. I'm sorry for giving you such a hard time. Please keep in touch – phone, e-mails. We shall miss you a lot.'

'You two mean the world to me. Thank you for everything. I'll contact you as soon as I arrive.'

I kiss mum on the cheek and then hug dad for a final time and make my way to the departure gates. I have to queue for a few minutes at passport control, but eventually hand over my passport before once more looking back and waving goodbye to my parents. Tears roll down my cheeks so I wipe my face and make my way to security.

Having got through security, I spend some time hanging around the duty free shops as I wait for information on my departure gate number. It's a twelve-hour flight so I go to the bookshop to peruse the shelves. Having purchased a book I wander back to the waiting area and watch the screen. The gate number finally appears and boarding is just over half an hour away, at four o'clock. Reality kicks in and I suddenly feel very alone. I take out my mobile phone and scroll through my contacts.

Who can I text or call? Perhaps I should text Rach or, even better, call Joe – tell him I'm at the airport. That will show him that I can do it. But what if he tries to change my mind? I can't call him. For God's sake woman, call Rachel instead!

I scroll between Rachel and Joe's numbers on my phone and then wonder why I haven't deleted his number.

Please call me now, Rach, to put me out of my misery and stop this nonsense!

I feel like screaming at the top of my voice.

Don't be bloody silly. I'm at the airport now. I can't turn back. Just move on. Read the book.

The boxing match continues inside my head for some time.

Maybe I should call Joe and tell him that I still love him. I can't do that! I mustn't do that!

I roll up one of my sleeves and I can see that the scar's still visible.

He did that. That womanising, cheating, abusive bastard did that. Why the fuck would I want to call him? I don't need him any more!

Tears are rolling down my cheeks so I get up and go to the toilets to splash some water on my face, wash my hands and look at my contacts list once more.

I need to get rid of that bloody number. I've found the courage to go to another country on my own, so surely I can find the courage to remove an unwanted number from my contact list? Then I'll be free of him for good.

And so I do it. I delete his number. The power he had over me has finally gone and it feels really good. I dry my face, pick up my belongings and walk out of the toilets towards the gate number, feeling a whole lot better about myself.

Time for a fresh start.

Part Two
Chapter Eight

'We will shortly be beginning our descent to Incheon Airport. Please ensure you stay in your seats and wear your seatbelts. Thank you for your attention,' says the voice through the speaker above my head.

A cabin attendant reaches my row, collecting rubbish from the passengers.

'Did you enjoy your Korean meal today?' she asks with a big smile on her face.

'Yes, I did,' I lie as she glances at the leftovers on my plate. 'The beef dish was nice. What was that really spicy side dish called again? It's really hot!' I add as I wave my hand in front of my mouth.

'Oh, you mean kimchi. Yes, it's very popular in Korea. It's eaten with almost everything.'

I thank her and she moves on to the row behind me.

As the plane descends, I'm eager to check out my new country from above. Fields, towns and cities pass by beneath us. The region looks to be quite rugged as I can see plenty of mountains on the horizon.

'You like view?' asks the elderly Korean man, who's sitting next to me and has been sleeping for nearly the entire journey.

'Yes, it looks impressive,' I reply, giving him a smile.

'Korea very mountain country,' he informs me. 'You see. Very good walk. Where you go?'

'I'm going to Seoul.'

'Very nice. Namsan mountain. Very nice. You see.'

I recall my father saying something about that mountain but I can't remember exactly what. 'Oh, yes. I really want to go there.'

'Here for holiday?' he asks.

'No, I'm going to work as an English teacher,' I answer. In my mind I can almost see the classroom of lovely, happy children that I'm going to teach.

'Oh. You teach me,' he says with a twinkle in his eye. 'Old man may be difficult for you. Bad student.' He laughs. 'You teach Hagwon?'

'Sorry, what's a Hagwon?' I ask, puzzled.

'I think you say language school.'

I recall seeing the word in the booklet that Colin sent me. 'Oh, of course. Yes, I am.'

A few minutes later the aircraft lands and the speaker switches back on. 'Ladies and gentlemen, we've now arrived at Incheon Airport. The local time is twelve-thirty pm and the weather is hot and cloudy with the possibility of a few heavy showers. The temperature is thirty degrees Celsius. Please make sure you take all your belongings with you and on behalf of British Airways we wish you a pleasant stay in South Korea.'

I have been warned about the humidity of the Korean summer and think I am wearing suitable clothing for the muggy conditions. The aircraft stops at its gate number so I unbuckle my belt and collect my belongings from the overhead compartment.

'Enjoy mountain and kimchi,' my elderly friend says. 'It's machusayo!'

'Oh, yes, the cabin attendant was telling me about that food earlier. What does machusayo mean – delicious?'

He laughs. 'Yes. You know one word. Welcome Korea. Few person speak English here so take care.' He wishes me luck and then joins the queue of people down the aisle. I wait for my chance to join the queue and try not to feel too impatient to get off the aircraft.

This is it. A brand new beginning and it's going to be a lot of fun!

After collecting my luggage and going through security, I walk towards the exit gates in great anticipation of what lies ahead. The doors open and I see a mass of people waiting behind the barriers, many of them are holding up pieces of paper scrawled with the names of passengers. I move towards the barrier and take a closer look to see if my name is among them, working my way down the line. The gabble of sound around me makes it difficult to concentrate on the task in hand.

'You want taxi? I take you!' offers a Korean taxi driver rather aggressively.

'I'm fine, thank you. I'm waiting for someone.'

I reach the end of the line without success and it's at this point that I'm suddenly awash with negative thoughts that have crept into my mind.

No sign with my name on it. Something isn't right, is it?

I put down my bags and search for the piece of paper with the details of the representative's contact name and number on it. Several minutes of calm searching turns into something more frantic as I can't remember where I put it. My panic begins to attract the attention of passers-by.

'Are you okay?' asks another Korean.

'I'm fine, thank you. I've just lost something. I'm sure I'll be fine,' I continue to scrabble around inside my bags for the important piece of paper.

'Okay. English not spoken by many person here so please take care,' he says.

You idiot, Charlotte! I can hear my mum's voice as I flap around looking for the bit of paper. Several minutes later, and without any joy, I give up.

What do I do now? It's far too early in the morning in the UK to phone Colin. I'll just have to sit it out and wait for the rep to turn up.

So that's what I do. I sit down and wait, and wait some more. As time passes by, I become increasingly anxious about my predicament. People come and go and I begin to develop hunger pains. I scan the airport building for somewhere to get some food and notice a familiar looking fast food restaurant that isn't too far away, so I pick up my bags and walk towards it. The smell of grilled burgers makes my taste buds go wild, so I order a burger and chips while keeping an eye out for someone looking for me. I pay with some of the Korean currency that my dad gave me at the airport and then return to where I was sitting before. The salty taste of the food leaves a lot to be desired and I still feel hungry after not eating much on the plane. As the minutes drag by and my contact still doesn't appear, I examine the contents of my bags once more but nothing turns up.

I'm not cut out for this. Just book a ticket on the next plane out of here and admit defeat.

Just as I'm about to give up hope, I spot a young-looking white man in his late thirties to early forties coming towards me. He has short brown hair, is wearing a smart black suit and is carrying a brown briefcase.

'Excuse me, are you Charlotte?' he asks, sounding somewhat uncertain.

'Yes, that's me.'

'Charlotte Dunn?'

I nod my head.

'Good. I thought it was you. I recognised you from the photo that Colin sent me.'

'Oh, yes, that's right. He wanted a photo of me but didn't say why,' I tell him, as the penny finally drops.

'My name's Chris and I am your representative. I'm very sorry about my lateness. We have a new driver and he doesn't seem to know his arse from his elbow. I had to direct him here – and he's supposed to be the bloody driver! Would you believe that he's Korean?' He shakes his head in frustration.

'Sounds like you're having a bad day too,' I say as we walk towards the car pick-up point.

'A bad day is an understatement! I shall call Colin later and let him know what a balls-up the whole operation has been. I know the guy's only been with us for a couple of weeks and that I should make allowances but I'll be recommending Colin to get rid of him. I doubt he'll do anything about it, though, as he hardly ever contacts me these days. He just lets me get on with it and ignores stuff he doesn't want to hear.' He pauses for thought. 'I'm sorry. It's just that I work out here alone. I suppose I shouldn't be telling you any of this.' He looks worried that he's let too many cats out of the bag to a relative stranger.

'Well, I'm sorry to hear about that,' I respond, trying to sound sympathetic.

This situation could be a whole lot better…

'I hope I haven't given off any bad vibes,' Chris goes on. 'It's not normally like this, I promise. Just a bad day, that's all.'

Okay, he's just having a bad day. We all have one of those once in a while, so give him a chance.

'How was your flight?' he asks, doing his best to change the subject.

'It was good, thank you, but now I feel really tired,' I answer as I cover a yawn.

'I can imagine. It's a long way. Have you eaten?'

'Yes, while I was waiting for you.'

'That's good. We have a busy schedule ahead of us,' he tells me.

Not the best of starts but he seems all right to me.

We leave the airport building and the humidity becomes all too apparent as a blast of hot air hits my face. A couple of minutes later we reach the car, where Chris's driver is waiting. Chris puts my luggage in the boot while I get in the back. Once Chris is in the car he tells me that we'll shortly be heading for Seoul.

The driver gets in behind the wheel.

'Charlotte,' says Chris, 'this is our driver, Mr Kim.'

Mr Kim turns around in his seat.

'Hello, Charlotte. Nice meet you.' He offers me his hand. I notice he's wearing a smart pair of black driving gloves.

'Nice to meet you too.'

We shake hands.

He's got a firm grip.

'My English no good. You thirsty? You have water.' He hands me a bottle.

That's thoughtful of him.

'Thank you very much.'

Mr Kim turns back, puts the key in the ignition and drives off. Gasping for a drink after the salty food I've just eaten, I open the bottle and gulp down nearly all of it in one go.

Minutes into the journey and the already fractured relationship between Chris and Mr Kim begins to surface.

'Mr Kim, I think you should've turned right not left at the last junction.'

The journey continues like this, with Chris repeatedly criticizing Mr Kim's apparent lack of sense of direction and Mr Kim barking back that it's his country and he knows where he's going.

Seems like Chris was right about him.

Eventually we find our way onto the highway and, according to Mr Kim at least, are making steady progress towards our destination, Seoul. Conversation peters out now there are fewer choices of route. I become aware of Mr Kim looking at me in his mirror and I notice for the first time a prominent scar running down the right side of his face. His gaze makes me feel uneasy as I shift around in the seat trying to get more comfortable.

Is he checking me out or something? Why is he smiling at me? Must stay awake but feel so sleepy. Need to focus on something. Try looking out of the window.

My vision starts to blur a little.

What's wrong with me? I feel strange. Probably just jet lag or something.

We pass through a landscape of rice fields and ugly high-rise apartments. The skies cloud over and spits and spots of rain sporadically hit the car windscreen. My eyelids are beginning to close and I'm drifting in and out of consciousness.

What's happening to me?

As I battle to keep my eyes open the two men start to talk to each other once more.

'Why are you turning off the highway?' asks Chris.

'This way quicker,' says Mr Kim, who seems determined to get his own way.

'But this way will take much longer.'

The surface of the road begins to break up a bit and I'm getting jolted about in the back seat.

'I don't think this is the best route at all,' Chris mutters.

'Silence! I am driver. This my country,' says Mr Kim forcefully.

Chris turns his attention to me, perhaps trying to diffuse the situation. 'It looks like the flight has caught up with you, Charlotte. Is everything okay back there?'

'Yes. Just very tired,' I mumble.

My eyes close again, only to flicker open a second later in response to a loud noise as the car takes a sharp turn.

What was that? Feel sick. Is he looking at me in the mirror again?

'Where are you going?' Chris demands. He sounds angry now. 'Why are you turning off the road? Go back, you idiot!'

I just about manage to look up and see that we've driven into a wooded area. A signpost in the distance jolts me from my somnolent state, but I'm unable to read it. Mr Kim stops the car and reaches for something inside his jacket.

'Get us back to the main road!' Chris orders. 'What the–?'

Is that a gun? Surely not.

'Be quiet! Do as I say and you no harm,' says Mr Kim, who's pointing a gun at Chris.

'Calm down. Why…' He pauses. 'Why are you doing this? I don't understand. Please don't hurt me!' Chris pleads in a shocked voice.

'Quiet!' repeats Mr Kim.

What's happening? Feel so sleepy.

'Can we come to some arrangement?' I hear Chris say in desperation. 'Is it money you want? I have plenty of it in my wallet. Take it all. I don't want to die!'

'I don't want money!' shouts Mr Kim.

Stay awake! Feel so useless…

'But – but what then? I don't understand,' Chris stammers.

'You don't need know why. Silence!'

Help me, Joe. I need you. Help me!

'I want girl. I give her sleeping pills.'

Pills? Did he just say he's given me pills?

'What? I don't understand you. You shouldn't have done that!'

'I tell you be quiet!'

'Let's just get her to the school and be done with it. We'll say no more about this–'

'I tell you shut up! Do what I say!' Mr Kim yells.

Joe, is that you? Feel so sleepy. Can't stay awake. Drifting…

Chapter Nine

When I finally awake it takes me some time to work out that I've been tied up, blindfolded and gagged. My throat is horribly dry and my head is spinning. I try to subdue the hysteria that threatens to overwhelm me.

What the hell's going on? Where am I? I don't think I'm in the car any more. Where's Joe – I mean, Chris?

I struggle to free my hands and feet, but I seem to be tied to a chair and it's nigh on impossible for me to move at all. Terrified almost out of my wits and very near to breaking point, I cannot begin to work out what's happening to me. It's useless struggling so at last I go still and wait for someone to come.

What feels like hours later, I hear footsteps approaching. There's the jangling sound of keys as a door is unlocked and my heart begins to race. I hear the door open and then shut and become aware that someone is standing somewhere close to me. I do not move. I hear a chair being pulled up towards me and then quietness descends once more.

Eventually a voice breaks the stillness.

'Ssssh!' it whispers.

The gag over my mouth is pulled down and I feel a cup being pushed against my bottom lip.

'Drink!' a man's voice orders.

The liquid touches my pursed lips and runs down my chin.

'Drink!' the stranger repeats a little louder.

I keep my lips firmly closed. A hand slaps my cheek hard. I give a short scream.

'Quiet!' the man yells. 'Here nobody hear you. Now drink!'

He squeezes open my bottom lip and pours the liquid down my throat. It's water. Some runs down my chin as

I'm forced to drink, but at least it quenches my raging thirst.

I try to speak. 'Who – who are you? Where am I?'

'Shut up and drink!'

After a couple more swallows, he pulls the gag up over my mouth and I hear him leave, locking the door on his way out. I try with all my might to scrape the rope against the chair, hoping that I can get my hands free like they do in the films, but I rock the chair too far and I go crashing to the floor, still securely trussed up. All I can do now is wait in a worse position than I was in before. Still feeling drowsy from the sleeping pills, I drift off back to sleep.

I'm awoken by the chair being put back upright. The gag is removed and I feel the cup being pressed against my bottom lip again.

'Drink!'

I sip the liquid this time without resisting. After a few seconds the cup is removed.

'Who are you?' I whisper. 'What do you want from me?'

'Shut up! You my property now. You no id, no friends.'

A shudder passes through my body.

'Nobody find you!' the man insists. 'You do everything I tell you!'

'Please let me go!' I beg in a tiny voice.

He pulls the gag back up over my mouth. I scream as loudly as I can behind it but the noise I make is pitifully feeble behind the cloth.

'No one can hear you.'

He sounds amused at my terror and helplessness, as though this was a sick game. He leans closer to me, enabling me to smell his stinky breath, and grips me underneath my chin.

I hear a click and feel something being pressed against my temple.

Oh my God, is that a gun?

'Mmm–mm!' I protest frantically through the gag.

'Don't make me angry!' the man shouts.

The pressing sensation disappears and the man goes away again, locking the door behind him. As I sob my heart out in silent despair I try to process everything that's happened.

Okay, stop crying, woman! What the hell is going on? How did I get here? Where's Chris? Is it best not to know? How am I going to get out of this?

No answers come to me. Hours later, unable to sleep, I hear the door being unlocked and someone come in. A light switch is being turned on, so I assume it's night time. Footsteps approach and I feel fingers undoing my blindfold. I blink as I take in my surroundings.

I am in a small, bare room. My captor is a craggy-faced Asian with jet black hair in, I estimate, his late forties or early fifties. He grabs the back of my head.

'You obey me now,' he hisses, revealing a number of gold teeth.

I nod my head.

'You do everything I tell you and no problem.' He strokes my hair, giving me the creeps.

I nod my head again, too scared to say anything.

He bends down and unties my hands and feet. 'Come with me,' he commands. 'Don't do stupid,' he warns me.

Seeing that I'm struggling to breathe, he removes the gag.

I get up, my joints aching and trembling after hours of inactivity. I lose my balance but he supports me by grabbing me around the waist and slowly walks me out of the room.

As we reach the doorway I try to scream for help but the merest squeak comes out of my mouth.

The man gives me a shake and lifts the gag up. 'You want this again?'

I shake my head obediently.

'Quiet! Nobody here save you,' he repeats.

He closes the door and leads me along a narrow corridor to another room, pushes me in and locks the door behind me.

Utterly bewildered, I survey my new surroundings. It's a shabby small room with one tiny window and a bed. I stumble over to the window, which has vertical metal bars across it, and look for any source of assistance, but it's too dark outside to see anything clearly. The only things I can identify are some building lights in the near distance that suggest that I'm quite high up.

How on earth am I going to get out of this alive?

I look for an escape route but there doesn't appear to be one. This high up, I realise, it's going to be difficult attracting someone's attention. I retreat to the bed and sink down onto the uncomfortable mattress. The only other object in the room is a bedside chest of drawers with the picture of Rachel and me placed on top.

What's that doing there?

Feeling a little bemused by it all I lie down and wait in the sticky heat of the night.

I'm not sure how much time has passed when I finally hear the door being unlocked. I sit up. My captor turns on the light and walks towards me, carrying a tray. He puts it down next to me. I'm paralysed with fear once more as he towers over me.

'Eat!' he orders.

I look inside the bowl. It's just rice. Nothing else. The only other thing on the tray is a glass of water.

'You work for me now,' the man says, staring at me. Then he smiles again, showing me his collection of gold teeth.

'Very pretty girl. Cheaper than Russian. You my prize.' Again he reaches out and strokes my hair. Then the smile vanishes. 'Tomorrow first night.'

He gets up and leaves the room, locking the door behind him as before.

I rush to the door and hammer on it. 'Please, why me?' I shout, sobbing. 'I've done nothing wrong! Let me go!'

There is no response.

Oh, God, what on earth does he mean? What are they going to do to me?

I stagger hopelessly back to the bed.

How could this have happened? Are Colin and Chris involved in all this? No, that doesn't make any sense. Chris only found out in the car. But is this why Colin wanted my picture? Oh, mum, you were right about me and my crazy notions. I should have listened to you!

I smack the mattress with the palm of my hand in frustration and despair.

Eventually I pick up the bowl of rice and examine it cautiously. I can't see anything wrong with it so I put some in my mouth and chew it slowly. It's tasteless, but seems to be okay. I shovel more into my mouth, then I pick up the glass of water and sniff it. It's odourless. I take a tentative sip. It tastes fine so I gulp down the rest.

Unable to do anything else, I rest my head on the bare mattress and eventually fall back to sleep.

Chapter Ten

Sensing someone's presence, I open my eyes quickly and see him staring down at me. I scream and try to move away from him but he grabs my neck. I try to wriggle free but he easily overpowers me.

'Don't make me angry!'

I stop wriggling and his tone of voice changes. 'You get good sleep?'

I catch a whiff of alcohol and stale cigarettes on his breath as he leans closer.

'No.' I start coughing as his stench works its way through my body.

'You don't like bed?' He sniggers. 'I pay good money for it so like.' The smell of alcohol intensifies as he leans closer still.

I'm guessing it would be unwise to displease this man.

'I give you nice room, I give you bed, now I give you breakfast. How about thank you?'

He touches my still sore cheek with his hand and that is enough for me to cooperate.

'Thank you,' I say shyly.

'Now eat rice and take bag. Later you wear clothes. Nice, sexy ones. Tonight first night.' He straightens up then leaves the room and locks the door.

I look inside the bag and take out a deep red sequined dress. I examine it in closer detail. It's a one-strap shoulder dress that's slanted at the bottom. I empty the bag and find a black G-string with a matching bra and a pair of fishnet stockings. I lie down on the bed and collect my thoughts.

That's it, then. I'm going to be working as a hooker.

I push the clothes away from me and eat my breakfast with automatic movements before lying down again and falling back to sleep.

Later on in the day I get up and look out of the window, which is a short distance away from my bed. It's tiny and makes me feel even more confined to this abysmal excuse for a room. It's a grey day outside. I can see a building being erected in the middle distance. Constructions workers are busily going about their business. I hear a siren and for a moment I have hopes that the police might already be on the case, but they are dashed just as quickly as I make out that it's an ambulance speeding along the road. With frustration mounting inside me, I sluggishly make my way back to my bed. I listen for sounds that might tell me more about my surroundings, but you could hear a pin drop in this seemingly empty building.

Just try to get some rest.

My tormentor returns that evening, wearing a smart black suit. He barks at me to take a shower and put on the clothes he gave me earlier. He leads me along the narrow corridor to a basic bathroom and waits outside while I do as he has ordered.

Once finished, I open the door and see my captor standing there. His gold teeth gleam as he looks me up and down. 'You look beautiful,' he tells me.

I tremble as I silently contemplate what might happen next.

'This for you,' he says, handing me another bag.

I look inside and find a pair of red stilettos and a make-up kit.

'Put on now!' he orders.

I go back into the bathroom and do as he has told me. Once I'm ready he grabs my arm and leads me out of the apartment. We head down several grubby flights of stairs.

'This all mine,' he boasts proudly. 'Nobody else here. But my dream to have people live in luxury apartment!'

Suddenly a couple of the jigsaw pieces in my head fall into place. He holds me around my waist, which makes me feel uneasy and consequently I stumble down a step, still getting used to the stilettos that I'm wearing, but he's there to keep me upright.

'Don't want injure you. You my special girl, make me many money.'

Once we reach the ground floor he walks me up to a big black door. He takes out his set of keys and before opening it, looks at me. 'No escape here. These door... all alarmed, all locked. No disappoint me. I know many people this city. They find you, no problem.'

His threat makes by blood run cold.

He opens the door and ushers me into a dark room beyond. I await my fate as he goes to turn the lights on.

'Welcome to Club Paradise,' says my captor. 'This my hostess club.'

He looks unbearably smug.

A faint smell of stale cigarettes invades my nostrils. I take in the décor, which is tired-looking and yellowish with cigarette smoke.

Paradise, this is not.

'You no like?' he asks, sensing something is amiss.

'It's nice. I like it.'

I hope that I have convinced him.

'Come, come. I show you.' He grabs me around my waist again and we walk into the bar together.

The circular bar, which occupies the centre of the room, is the main focal point. The floor is covered with red carpet with a few stains on it. There are also a few small tables and bar chairs dotted around. Along the sides of the room are seating booths fitted out with long, burgundy curtains that can be drawn for greater privacy.

No booths over there in that corner though. I wonder what that's all about?

We cross to the other side of the club, where there's an inner door. My captor ensures that I'm not looking as he taps in the numbers for the door. He pushes the door open and gestures at me to go in.

'This my office,' he announces proudly. 'Sit here.'

I sit down opposite him, feeling nervous. There is a laptop on the table along with a lamp and what looks like a girly calendar from where I'm sitting. There is another door directly behind him. I wonder where it leads.

'You like my office?'

I nod my head mutely.

'The other girl come soon.'

He gets up and walks to the window, through which he can see into the club itself. He pulls the blinds up and admires his empire for a moment or two, then comes back to me.

'Get up!' he orders.

I jump up and turn to face him. He grabs my arms, pulling me towards him and looking me in the eyes. His devilish face is the epitome of all things evil.

'The Korean girl, their English no good. Don't talk to girl. You talk to girl, you talk to client about you, life finish. Understand?'

I shiver all over and nod my head.

'Some rule you must to know. You work every night. You keep customer happy. Pour drink, smile. Customer want you sing song, you sing song. Customer want happy time, you give happy time.'

Whatever does he mean by that?

'This your job. I pay you no money. You live here free so money no need. I feed you. I care you. Our secret. You keep customer happy, understand?'

I nod my head once more.

He seems satisfied that I understand. 'Good. Open one hour. Girl come soon. Go! Wait outside for customer.'

I stumble out of his office and sit down at a shabby-looking booth, barely having time to gather my thoughts before the main door is unlocked and another man walks into the room. My captor comes out of his office to greet him. They speak, then my captor turns and beckons me over.

'This my number two,' he explains. 'Call him Mr Yi. Maybe you already meet.'

What's he on about?

Mr Yi doesn't break into a smile. He has a stocky frame and I can tell from his muscular build that he probably works out every day. Then I register the scar that runs down from the top of his right cheek bone to his chin.

He was the driver!

My captor fixes me with a rigid stare. 'Mr Yi watch and listen everything. Make no mistake. Don't fuck with me!'

I glance back at Mr Yi. He drives his clenched fist silently into the palm of his right hand. I quiver and break out in a cold sweat.

It wasn't meant to be like this! How could it have ended up like this?

My captor gives a grunt. 'I busy now. Mr Yi care you. Girl come soon.'

He heads off while I try to catch my breath, which isn't easy with Mr Yi glaring at me. All I can do is sit back down and wait for the girls to arrive.

The main double doors open again and the girls walk in, accompanied by a short middle-aged man, who goes straight to the bar and immediately starts polishing glasses. I count twenty girls in total. My captor walks over to them then leads the chattering, giggling bunch in my direction.

He makes an announcement to the girls, presumably explaining who I am. They all start to speak to me at the same time in what I can only assume is Korean. I rack my brains to work out what they are saying.

Nope. I don't even know the basics of the language. It's useless!

'Hello. Nice to meet you,' is all I can manage.

This seems to amuse the girls and some of them laugh and giggle uncontrollably.

Great. I'm working with a bunch of airheads who know zilch. That's all I need.

Then I notice that there's some whispering going on between one of the girls, who seems different in some way to the others, and my captor. My captor introduces her to me.

'This is Mi-Young,' he tells me.

We look at each other. She's wearing a figure-hugging one-piece red dress that shows off her curvaceous body.

She looks a bit older than the rest. I wonder what her job is?

'She manage other girl,' my captor adds helpfully.

She takes a step closer. 'Hello. My English no good.' She doesn't offer her hand and she isn't smiling. 'Other girl cannot help you. They no speak English. Do job well and no problem,' she advises me coldly.

She stares daggers at me and I sense she will be no friend to me.

How much does she know about my situation? Is she in on this too?

My captor addresses all of the girls and they all bow to him and say something in reply, but I have no idea what is being said.

Mi-Young taps my arm sharply. 'Bow to him,' she demands.

I do so, copying the others.

Mi-Young looks unimpressed. 'We open soon. Your work begin now. Sit down and I bring customer to you.'

Within minutes a trickle of Asian men start making their way into the club. I count around fifteen. Most are middle-aged. Some have come in groups, while others appear to be alone. Most of them seem to be wearing their work clothes, all suited up. I look around and can see that the place isn't overly busy.

Mi-Young welcomes more new arrivals and escorts them to their tables, where the girls are seated waiting for them. I observe what the girls closest to me are doing. Some of the girls seem to be on good terms with their customers and smile sweetly at them and laugh whenever something is said to them. They also pour drinks for their guests. The room is now just under half-full and I realise that most of the girls are now busy, with some guests having more than one girl by their side.

Surely it'll be my turn soon.

Moments later Mi-Young clocks me and my empty table and comes my way with a customer.

This is it.

She gestures at me to stand up so I do so.

'Make Mr Lee welcome,' she instructs me.

Mr Lee is an averagely built man in his mid to late fifties with jet black hair. He's wearing glasses and a dark suit. As he approaches he scans me up and down. Then a big smile lights up the whole of his face.

'He very important client,' she warns me. 'He want you to sing English song. I get microphone.'

She deposits a large green bottle and a glass on the table and apparently invites him to take a seat next to me. We both sit down. I glance at the bottle and wonder what's in it. He makes himself comfortable, moving his chair very close to mine, which makes me feel vulnerable. He holds his empty glass up and looks at me expectantly. I pick up the bottle and pour liquid into his glass, spilling some of its contents on the table.

'I'm sorry,' I mumble.

'No problem. My English very bad. What you name?' he asks with interest.

I tell him. He looks at me longingly and gives me a toothy grin. 'I like name. I like white girl, especially British girl. You beautiful in red dress. You sing song good?'

He gulps down his drink so I pour him another. 'Yes, I can sing for you,' I reply reluctantly.

'Aww. Good. Very happy.'

'What would you like me to sing?'

'Beatle. I like Beatle song.'

Mi-Young returns and hands me the microphone and the karaoke remote control.

'Everything okay?' Her dagger-like stare tells me that there is only one acceptable answer to her question.

'Yes, everything's fine,' I tell her.

She leaves us alone to look after another client, who is waiting for her at the bar.

'Which song would you like me to sing?' I ask him.

'Yesterday. Beatle song,' he replies, taking another large gulp of his drink.

I find the song on the remote and tap the number into the machine.

What am I doing? Am I really about to sing a Beatles song under threat to a group of complete strangers, whose response to me I cannot possibly predict? How is this happening? All I can do is give it my best shot and hope for the best...

I begin to sing and try to think of nothing but making a good job of it. My nerves start to settle. He looks at me intently while I sing away and smiles. I finish the song at last and lay the microphone down. To my surprise a number of people sitting at the bar start clapping.

'You sing good,' he says.

He looks at me adoringly and then places a hand on my thigh. I cringe.

What does he think he's doing?

I move my leg away and this seems to displease him. His smile evaporates and is replaced by a look of perplexed irritation.

'I pay good money talk you! Do you want me complain?' he demands angrily.

That gets me flustered. 'No, no – Please don't do that. I'm sorry!'

He takes a long drink then puts his glass down. 'Don't anger me again,' he warns me.

'I'm sorry. I won't.'

What a creepy, horrid man! Better not piss him off, though. Heaven knows what the consequences might be.

His expression softens again. 'Please sing more song.'

I put on a fake smile and notice that his glass is almost empty so I top it up before choosing another Beatles number. At the end he applauds me and replaces his hand on my thigh. This time I let it be.

'So what are your hobbies?' I enquire shakily, trying in desperation to ignore the pressure of his hand.

'Hobbies?' he echoes. 'I like baseball very much,' he says after a moment's thought.

'Oh, I don't know much about baseball because it's not very popular in the UK. Which team do you support?' I ask, trying to distract him.

'I like LG Twins. They number one team in Seoul.'

He removes his hand from my thigh and takes a large swig of his drink. My ploy seems to have worked. 'Like team for long time. Many year ago I go all time with father,' he continues, reminiscing mistily about his past.

If daddy could just see his little boy right now…

'Which team are their main rivals?' I ask, recalling what Joe used to say about Tottenham Hotspur's greatest rivals, Arsenal, and the importance of winning the derby matches.

'What mean? Sorry my English very bad,' he replies, looking bemused.

'I mean two teams that really don't like each other,' I explain.

'I see. You good teacher!' He laughs out loud. 'That's Doosan Bears. We hate each other so – yes, we rivals.' He picks up his glass and gulps down some more alcohol then hands me the microphone. 'Please sing Beatle song.'

He really does like them.

I tap in another number and launch into 'Hey Jude'.

After I've performed a whole string of more Beatles songs he draws my attention to the label on the green bottle. 'This drink soju. Very strong. Everyone Korea drink. Made from – forget name. My English worse after drink this.' His face is now bright red so he loosens his tie and unbuttons his collar.

You've definitely had one too many, Mr Lee.

He can't maintain focus any more and his breath reeks. He places his hand on my thigh again but I choose to ignore it rather than risk provoking his temper again.

Finally he staggers to his feet. 'I go now but tonight enjoy very much. I want see you again.'

Great, now I have a stalker on my hands.

I catch a glimpse of Mi-Young watching my every move as he leans over to kiss me on the cheek. She does not make any move to intervene as the touchy-feely Mr Lee starts to paw me. Then, however, he loses interest and wobbles off towards Mi-Young and the exit, talking to her briefly before disappearing into the night.

Mi-Young looks at me then glides across the floor in her black stilettos. Many of the clients sitting at the circular bar watch as she makes her majestic way across to me. She clearly knows they are watching her and flicks her hair back as she acknowledges the guests nearest to her.

It's pretty obvious who really runs the show here.

'Good job,' she tells me coolly, her smile disappearing almost as soon as it has appeared. 'Mr Lee happy.' She gives me a stern look. 'Don't fail me. Always keep client happy. Now I find you more client. Sing more song.'

I nod and she walks away again, her hips swaying seductively from side to side.

Other clients come and go all night. Some stay for a long time, asking inane questions, while others don't stay as long because they find it far too difficult to converse in English. They all have one thing in common, however: they all enjoy listening to me singing the Beatles.

As the night goes into the early hours, the clients begin to venture back home and I notice that the ones who are still around are being entertained by more than one woman. Mi-Young comes over once more and barks orders at me to sing until the bar closes.

While I'm singing, I see one of the girls take a client's hand and lead him to the other side of the bar and into a booth, where the long red curtains hide them from view. I keep an eye on the booth and lose my place in the song, but nobody seems to be listening much any more, apart from Mi-Young, who's still monitoring my every move. The remaining clients are all either sloshed or engaged in fondling the hostess girls.

The song finishes and I take stock for a moment.

What is going on over there? Maybe this is really no more than a massage parlour after all. Try not to think about it.

Twenty minutes later the two re-emerge. The girl leads the client to the door and he kisses her on the cheek. I see Mi-Young go over to where the few remaining clients are and say something to them. Money changes hands and a couple of the hostess girls give them their coats and they leave.

First night over and done with. Mr Lee gives me the creeps but what can I do about it?

The hostess girls help clear away the glasses and Mi-Young orders me to help. Finally the place looks tidy and she allows the other girls to go home. They collect their belongings, laughing and giggling away to each other like they don't have a care in the world. There are now just the three of us in the room. I am ushered over to where Mi-Young and Mr Yi are sitting. Mi-Young picks up her phone and makes a call.

What's happening now?

I wait in tense silence for fifteen minutes, then my captor comes into the room. He helps himself to a drink from the bar, then sits down with us. He converses briefly with Mi-Young and Mr Yi. Mi-Young gets up, bows to both men and leaves the building. Mr Yi locks the door behind her and comes back.

Is Mi-Young in on this or not?

'You meet Mr Lee,' my captor says to me.

I nod my head.

'He very important client. He like you.' He puts his hand on mine and begins to squeeze it, gradually increasing the pressure. He looks into my eyes. 'Anything he want you give, understand?'

Scared witless, I nod my head obligingly and he lets go of my hand. I glance down at it and see that the skin is a ghostly white, where he had been pressing it.

'Now I take you back to room.'

The two men escort me to my room without speaking, push me in, and lock the door. I hear them speaking to each other outside in the corridor for a while and then everything goes quiet. I plonk myself down on the bed.

Fucking mattress. Hard as nails.

I lie down and try to consider the situation.

How on earth am I ever going to escape from this?

Chapter Eleven

'I've been thinking about what you said earlier and I don't want to put you off or anything…' says Liz as she breaks off to add a spoonful of sugar to her coffee.

'Go on,' I reply, urging her to spit it out.

She takes a sip of her coffee. 'It's just a friend of mine taught English in Japan and the school failed to pay her salary as the business was going under.'

'Oh? Did she manage to get her money back in the end?'

'No. She had to borrow some money to get by until she could find another job.'

'Do you think I should still give it a try?' I ask, worried.

'Oh, yeah. Just be careful.' She shoots me a reassuring smile.

We finish our coffees and get back to stacking the shelves on the supermarket floor.

If only she had told me to give it a miss.

The unlocking of the door unnerves me. My captor walks in, bringing the same food for breakfast as he did yesterday. He dumps the tray on the bed.

'Eat,' he instructs me.

I sit up, survey the offerings, and push the tray to one side.

He puts his hand behind my head and applies some pressure, making me yell.

'Eat!' he orders. 'You must eat. Don't want sick girl. No good for me, understand?'

I pull the tray closer and pick up the spoon, then start shovelling cold rice into my mouth. Seeing that I'm cooperating, he releases his grip.

'Much better. Tonight Mr Lee come. He want see you. Look beautiful, yes?'

I nod my head.

He gets up, tells me that he'll be back later and then locks the door. All I can do is sit and wait.

The time passes by so slowly that my mind begins to wander. I look around the room for something to relieve the stultifying boredom creeping over me but find I'm high and dry. Suddenly a thought crosses my mind.

I should be recording the number of days I'm stuck here.

I examine the wall, which does not appear to have seen a lick of paint for years. Then I search for something sharp. I find a loose nail under my bed and use it to scratch two lines to show the number of days I've been stuck in this godforsaken hole. Then I lie back on the ungiving mattress and go back to sleep, hoping to dream of exotic far-flung places filled with friends, fun and laughter.

Instead I dream of when I was with Joe.

In my dream I'm very excited because Joe is taking me out to celebrate my twentieth birthday. He's refusing to tell me where we're going exactly, though I do know he has booked a table at a fancy restaurant somewhere.

'This is gonna be a really special night, babe,' he promises me, rubbing his hands together.

'So come on then, spill the beans. Where are you taking me?'

'Don't you worry – all will be revealed in good time,' he says enigmatically.

We buy our tickets and get on a train headed for London Euston.

'Ooh, so you're taking me to London?'

'Well, I know how much you like musicals so I thought I would buy some tickets.' He opens his wallet and waves some theatre tickets in my face.

'What are those tickets for?' I ask, trying to grab them off him.

'Just you wait!' he replies, putting the tickets back in his wallet.

'Oh, Joe, you're such a tease!'

We get off the train and make our way to the underground station.

'Come on, this is our stop,' he tells me, leading me off the train at Leicester Square.

'Isn't the West End around here?'

He rolls his eyes at me. 'Did you leave your brains on the train? Of course it bloody well is!'

'Okay, Joe, I was only asking.' I can't help feeling a little hurt by his comments.

Minutes later we are sitting down in a beautiful Thai restaurant, waiting to be served dinner. Joe orders a lager and I ask for a glass of red wine.

'Oh, Joe, this place is so authentic. Look at the carving on the tables. It's like we're in Thailand together. Let's go there one day.'

'That'd be nice,' he says, slipping his hand over mine.

The waitress arrives with the drinks and Joe picks up his glass and takes a large swig.

'Go easy,' I say reprovingly. 'We've got a long night ahead of us.'

He ignores me and takes a second gulp in quick succession. 'I know my own body, for God's sake!'

After our meal, we walk to the theatre.

'So what are we going to see?' I ask him.

We turn the corner and he points towards a building ahead of us. I look at the huge poster that's lit up by neon lights on the side of the building.

'Oh, Joe! *Les Misérables*!' I exclaim as I embrace him. I am blissfully happy.

'I just want to make it a special day for you,' he tells me, holding my hand.

We queue up to enter the building and take our seats close to the stage.

'Wow, you must have paid a lot for these seats!' I whisper, unable to hide my surprise.

'Only the best for you, babe.'

At the interval he tells me he's going to the toilet. The second act begins but there is no sign of him so I get up from my seat and go in search of him. I wait outside the men's toilets for a while, but he does not appear.

Maybe he's gone to the bar?

I make my way there and find him sitting on a stool with a pint in his hand.

'Joe? Are you okay?'

'What are you doing here?' he asks abruptly. 'Why aren't you watching the show?'

'I want to watch it together.'

'In all honesty, it's boring as hell and I'd rather have a pint,' he replies as he sups his drink.

'But it's my birthday!'

He shrugs. 'So just go back in there and enjoy it and come here after it's finished.'

Now he's making me angry. 'Thank you very much!' I exclaim bitterly. 'You've ruined our evening.'

He takes another drink. 'In that case, we might as well leave now.'

'Fine!' I retort.

He finishes his drink and we leave the theatre in silence. As we walk down a quiet street outside I see a bin and stride towards it.

'I was going to keep this as a souvenir,' I say, brandishing the ticket before chucking it in the bin.

'I'm sorry, babe, but I really wasn't enjoying it. Why don't we find a hotel?' he suggests, putting his arm around me.

'I just want to get home – and you're drunk!' I'm really annoyed with him.

'It's always about you, isn't it?' he snaps back. 'What about me for once?'

'Have you forgotten it's my birthday?'

'I know you really want me,' he says as he pats my bottom, then slides his hand up my skirt.

'Stop it!' I protest as I struggle to push him away.

He's much stronger than me and pushes me up against the wall.

'Shut up. You know you want it,' he mutters as he starts kissing my neck.

'No, I don't! What's got into you?'

All of a sudden he grabs me, causing me to lose my balance and fall heavily to the ground. My arm is trapped under my body and I scream in pain. My eyes are blurred with tears as I look down and see that my arm is covered with blood and that there's a broken bottle on the floor. He bends down to pick me up.

'Wake up! Wake up!'

I open my eyes and realise I'm being violently shaken by Mr Yi.

Seeing that face and the awful scar makes me scream even louder as I lash out at him. It's all in vain, however, as he has me pinned down to the bed. I struggle to breathe properly and at the same time realise I'm drenched with sweat.

'What wrong?' Mr Yi demands, still pinning me down – seemingly his attempt at trying to calm me down. Being trapped like this just makes me feel ten times worse so I try to wriggle free, but it's useless. I take a couple of deep breaths and my heart rate slows down.

'You bad dream?' he asks, puzzled.

Trembling violently, I avoid looking directly up at him.

'I'm cold,' I mumble. 'Could I have some bed linen?'

He looks at me with bewilderment, then lets go of me and stands up.

'Shower and get ready. Bar open one hour,' he bellows.

My second night begins at the hostess bar. The other girls arrive together, laughing and giggling amongst themselves, just like they did last night. They don't seem to notice me sitting alone at the table. Only Mi-Young pays me any attention, gliding over to give me this evening's instructions.

'Mr Lee come soon. I send him to you. Keep him happy,' she says, without even asking how I am.

The bar opens for the evening and the men pile in.

This place is much busier than last night.

The girls, who have been laughing and giggling since they arrived, disperse around the room and begin entertaining their clients. Mi-Young brings over my first client. She hands me the microphone and tells me to sing to him. I pour him a drink and start on the music.

'Have you had a good day today?' I ask during a pause as I rest my voice.

He looks at me blankly and I sense that he's unable to understand let alone utter a word in English. Instead he gets up and wanders off in Mi-Young's direction, which unnerves me.

Shortly afterwards Mi-Young comes over to speak to me.

'He say that he feel uncomfortable around you. What you do?' she demands.

'All I asked him was if he was having a good day.'

She glares at me. 'I told you sing to him. He no speak English and now he gone because of you!'

'Sorry, Mi-Young. It won't happen again,' I mumble apologetically.

Her face comes up closer to mine. 'I watch you,' she says through gritted teeth. Then, maintaining her composure, she turns and glides off back to the bar, watched as usual by all the men.

Mi-Young reappears some time later with Mr Lee in tow.

'Hi, Charlotte,' says my admirer, smiling broadly. 'Good to see you again.'

Mi-Young takes his jacket while he sits down and looks at the drinks menu. She comes back, writes down his drink order and goes to the bar.

He looks at me intently, giving me the creeps. 'I think about see you tonight all day,' he tells me. He keeps smiling as he places his hand on my thigh. 'I want you sing song tonight. 'Love me do' by Beatle.' He looks at me longingly and it triggers something deep inside.

I find myself wanting Joe to be around right now, which makes my stomach churn even more as I recall the dream I had this afternoon. My mood worsens but I know I can't show this, so I put on a fake smile and try not to tremble when he starts stroking my thigh.

Mi-Young comes back with his drink and puts it on the table in front of us. My hand shakes as I pick up the glass and pour him some soju, once again spilling some of it on the table.

He laughs. 'Yesterday same. Need more practice. I want you sing.'

He takes his hand off my thigh and downs his soju in one while I find the song and tap in the number.

Once I have finished singing, I put down the microphone and he draws closer.

'You sing song well. Give me more soju.' He loosens his tie and unbuttons his collar. 'I tell you about me. I work for big company in Korea. Management level. This my way for relax after long day.' He gulps down some soju, replaces the glass on the table and wipes his mouth with the back of his hand.

'How long have you been coming here?' I ask quietly.

'Long time. I very important customer. Many money spend Paradise.' He gazes at me. 'I very happy you here.

I ask many time for white girl come.' He finishes off his soju and I pour him another.

'Why do you like white girls so much?'

'Beautiful girl. White skin, blonde hair, blue eyes.'

He holds his hand out and begins to stroke my hair. I want to back away but in the corner of my eye I see Mi-Young watching me with her steely eyes.

'So beautiful girl,' he murmurs.

I shiver all over as he carries on touching my hair. Then he picks up his glass and concentrates upon the other love in his life, knocking back the clear, pungent liquid.

The night goes on with me singing songs by the Beatles and other British bands from the same era. There are brief interludes during which he tells me more about his life. The more he drinks, the more I dislike him. He starts talking about his private life and tells me that he's married with two young children but that he rarely gets to see his family due to the long hours that he works.

'Sunday is family day,' he explains.

I feel no sympathy for him whatsoever. I ask him why he comes here after work. He tells me it's how he relaxes.

'I go soon,' he says at last. 'Busy day tomorrow. Tonight enjoy.' He runs his hand up and down my thigh. I shudder and feel that I'm being violated.

'Want more,' he mutters.

What does he mean by that?

He gets up and nearly falls over. 'Too much alcohol,' he tells me. Spotting his trip, Mi-Young rushes over to check that he's okay. She then gets his jacket and helps him put it on. He whispers something to her and they both look at me. She nods her head and then he walks with her to the door.

What did he say to her?

I feel drained at this point and rest my head on my hands. I want to run off to the toilet to cry but force myself to stay where I am.

'I bring more customer. Smile!' Mi-Young commands, coming over to me and giving me a demonstration of how it's done properly.

Sarcastic bitch!

She wanders off to find some more clients for me. Unable to hold the tears in, I take the opportunity to go to the toilet. Mi-Young spots me so I point to where I'm going and she nods her head curtly but points at her wrist, suggesting it should be just a short break.

I open the toilet door and find a hostess girl inside busily washing her hands. She looks up at me and giggles, dries her hands and glides out in her high heels.

When the bar finally closes and the hostess girls have gone home I'm escorted back to my room by Mr Yi, feeling absolutely shattered by the night's events. He locks me in my makeshift cell for the night and I collapse onto the bed.

It's only as I close my eyes that it occurs to me that I haven't seen my captor all night. Then I drift off to sleep.

Chapter Twelve

'Sit here,' barks Mi-Young the following evening as I brace myself for another night's work. She seems grumpier than usual. 'I come back later,' she tells me before stalking off in the direction of the office.

I sit down at my usual place and am waiting for the bar to open when all of a sudden my captor and Mi-Young storm out of the office. There's evidently a bit of a commotion going on with raising of voices and vigorous nodding of Mi-Young's head. The other girls have yet to arrive so only I and Mr Yi are present to witness the heated exchange. My captor snatches up his jacket and a big black bag, then goes to the bartender's cash till, opens it and removes a huge wad of notes, which he waves about in the air while shouting his head off. Then he stuffs the money in his bag and walks to the exit, which he slams shut behind him. Mr Yi, looking as menacing as ever, takes his post beside it, guarding this hellhole as though nothing's happened.

What was all that about? Money troubles, maybe?

Mi-Young comes towards me and shouts at the top of her voice in Korean.

What have I done?

She stands over me. 'No mistake tonight, okay?' she yells.

'But–'

'Quiet! Be nice Mr Lee. He very important customer. Understand?'

The hairs on the back of my neck stand up and I shiver all over.

'Yes, yes, of course.'

The door opens and the hostess girls wander in, seemingly blissfully unaware that anything unpleasant is going on behind the scenes in this murky establishment.

Airheads, the lot of 'em!

Mi-Young puts on her big smile and greets them. I feel utterly alone.

Is anyone out their searching for me yet?

As the night wears on Mr Lee rears his ugly head once more. I see him being welcomed by Mi-Young on the other side of the room.

I wonder what they're talking about? She usually brings him straight over.

Eventually she shows him to his seat at my table with a tray of drinks, places them on the table and leaves us to it.

'I've missed you,' he tells me as he sits down.

Can't say the same about you.

I pour him his usual drink and he picks up the glass and takes a huge swig.

'Today so busy. Work hard all day. No break. Very tired. Sing song to me. Make me better.' Then he puts his hand on his crotch and starts rubbing vigorously.

God, you make me sick!

A couple of hours pass by and Mr Lee is much the worse for wear. He is drunk, dishevelled and mumbling, making even less sense than he usually does. I'm distracted for a moment by something going on over the other side of the room. I see a hostess girl pour a drink over a client's head. An argument breaks out between the two of them. Mr Yi rushes over to remove the man from the bar. The client thrashes his arms around in a drunken fashion but Mr Yi's strength wins out in the end.

Mr Lee grabs my hand and I suddenly find myself focusing on my own problem.

'You…' He pauses. 'You make alive, Charlotte,' he mutters through the drink.

I try to deflect his train of thought. 'What about your wife? Don't you love her?'

He looks agitated. 'I no see her much.'

I try to keep his mind on other things. 'Why don't you go home now and see her?'

'No!' he barks. 'Stay here you!'

His cheeks redden and I suddenly feel uneasy. Mi-Young clocks me, casting her beady eye over the situation and heads in our direction.

'Okay, calm down,' I mutter, trying to appease him. 'How about another drink?'

'I don't want drink! I want...' His voice trails off.

Before he can resume what he's saying, Mi-Young appears at his elbow. They chat for a little while and then he nods his head, gets up and allows her to lead him over to a spare table next to mine.

Oh God, he's complained to her. I'm done for!

After a word or two more, however, the pair return to my table and he seems to be in a better mood. He sits down again and Mi-Young hovers nearby, checking that all is well again.

Best not ask what's been said...

'More drink?'

I pour him another and he downs it in one go. Mi-Young seems satisfied and leaves us to attend to some other clients, who have just entered the bar.

'No talk about wife again,' he tells me abruptly. 'Make me angry.'

I nod my head. 'I'm sorry. I won't, I promise. How about I sing more songs?'

He grunts assent so I pick up the microphone and sing some of his requests. Eventually his mood changes as he becomes more relaxed, though he's still extremely drunk. He slurs his words and is barely audible but eventually I make out 'hungry' and 'go home' and realise he's going. He stands up and leans towards me, then whispers something in my ear, but I can't understand any of it.

Mi-Young comes over with Mr Lee's jacket, with Mr Yi in tow. Together they help him off the premises.

The evening ends and all the other hostess girls leave too until it's just Mi-Young, Mr Yi and the hostess girl, who caused a few problems earlier left behind.

I wonder what's going to happen to her?

My captor arrives back at the club, looking harassed. He chats to Mi-Young for some time but his manner is more composed than it was earlier. After they have finished their discussion he walks up to the hostess girl with Mr Yi and starts to shout at the poor girl, bellowing every word at her. My body tenses as I see him slap her. She starts to cry, drops to the floor and pleads with him for forgiveness but he only slaps her again repeatedly. She screams and is obviously in considerable pain. Mi-Young watches and does nothing. Eventually Mr Yi grabs the girl's belongings, picks her up and chucks her out through the exit, throwing her coat and bag onto the pavement outside.

Guess she won't be coming back again.

A minute or two later, Mi-Young puts on her coat and leaves the bar and Mr Yi locks the main door behind her.

Then my captor strides over towards me, beetroot red in the face, and grabs me, pulling me off my seat onto the floor and shouting at me. I yelp in terror and surprise.

'You make Mr Lee angry, you make me angry! Understand?' he screams.

The two men tower over me menacingly.

'I'm sorry, I'm sorry!' I plead.

'Don't talk about wife again!'

'I promise I won't. Never ever again!' I'm utterly terrified by now.

That bitch!

I feel my captor's breath on my skin and the all too familiar waft of soju billowing from him. He raises his hand to hit me. I try to wriggle free.

'Please don't hurt me!'

Somehow he stops himself from hitting me, perhaps not wanting to injure his prized asset. Instead he pulls my head closer to his. The smell of soju is overpowering.

'You see what I do to girl? She can be replace. Many girl want work here. Other girl come tomorrow, no problem…' He pauses. 'Mr Lee still like you so lucky girl but make him angry, I punish you! Mr Lee like you so give yourself him. He pay good money!'

My captor throws me down in a fit of rage and I burst out crying. He shouts at me in Korean and raises his arm as though he's about to slap me but again the blow doesn't land. Instead he rants at Mr Yi, who responds by throwing me over his shoulder and carrying me upstairs to my cell. He deposits me on the bed and then, without a word, stomps out and turns the key in the door.

Feeling utterly helpless and with a pounding headache, I cry until there are no tears left.

Someone out there has to be looking for me by now! Please, dad. Anyone! Help me!

Chapter Thirteen

I'm in my usual place when the doors open the following evening. The hostess girls come in together to start their evening shift. A quick glance at the girls and I notice a new girl, who's all alone at the back of the room. I see that she isn't conversing with any of the others, who are being their usual silly selves.

She seems different to the rest of them.

The new girl looks across at me and smiles. Something awakens my dulled senses for the first time in a while.

She's noticed me! Someone's actually noticed me for once!

A few minutes later the clients start pouring in.

It really is getting so much busier in here.

I hold my breath waiting to see if *he* is there.

Phew! No sign of Mr Lee, nor of my captor, thank God.

I almost feel like smiling but then remind myself that lately my captor has not arrived till later in the evening.

I glance across at the table next to me, where the new girl is waiting for her first client. I manage to make eye contact with her for a split second and we both smile, then she looks away.

Just being nice to me?

Mi-Young walks over with my first client for the evening. He's a fragile old man in an even older, grubby-looking suit. He sits down next to me, smelling of stale cigarettes.

'He want hear song,' Mi-Young informs me. 'He like voice.' Then she goes off to get the man his drink.

'I no here for long time,' he says while settling in his chair.

'Why is that?' I ask inquisitively.

'I work at factory near bar but close last year.'

Mi-Young returns with his drink which he takes from her and gulps down. He places the half-empty glass on the table and continues his story.

'Before many many people here but now no so many.'

I look around me and see that the place is relatively lively.

'But it's pretty busy this evening.' I tell him.

He puffs out his cheeks. 'This no busy like before. Many worker come here but factory close and factory worker go other bar. Only one factory open here. Itaewon popular today.' He looks at me. 'You no sound Russian. Where from?'

'I'm from the UK.'

'Hmm. Russian girl here before.' He picks up his glass and takes a swig before putting it back down on the table. 'That why come today. Friend tell me that new white girl here again. You speak Korean? English so difficult for me.' He raises his forearm to his face, which is drenched in sweat, and gives it a quick wipe.

'No, I don't.'

He looks disappointed.

'Many Russian girl speak some Korean. It more easy for me.' He looks like he has found a penny but lost a pound for a moment before picking up his glass again and finishing off his drink. He calls Mi-Young over to order another one.

Sensing that I'm not going to glean much more from him I change tack. 'What song would you like me to sing?'

For Christ's sake, don't say the bloody Beatles!

An hour or so passes by slowly and still I'm stuck with this old man, who is so drunk that he's slouched on the table. The new girl at the next table is in a similar position to me. She glances at me and smiles as if she understands my predicament.

86

She definitely seems different to the rest. She could be my way out of here. I must talk to this girl – but how? Where can we go that's private? The ladies room! I just need to go to the toilet when she gets up. Other girls go at the same time so it should be fine.

My chance comes some fifteen minutes later. The other girl's client leaves so she gets up and heads for the toilet. The elderly gentleman I'm with is practically asleep and Mi-Young is busy talking to a client so I take my opportunity to slip quietly away and talk to the girl.

I steal into the ladies room.

She must be in one of the two cubicles – and the other one is free!

I nip into the vacant cubicle and sit and wait. I hear the toilet next door being flushed and the cubicle door unlocks so I quickly do the same. We meet by the wash basin.

'Hi,' I say in a friendly manner.

'Hi. I'm Francesca,' she replies as she dries her hands on a paper towel and then turns towards me. Her smile reveals a set of perfect, pearly white teeth. Her porcelain skin and svelte figure leads me to think that she could be a very popular girl at this place.

'Nice to meet you. I'm Charlotte.'

'Nice to meet you too.'

She can speak English. Yes! Ask her a question.

'I hope you don't mind me asking, but where are you from?' I enquire hesitantly.

'Why you ask?' I sense some mistrust.

'It's just I feel that you're not from Korea, that's all. Am I right?'

'Okay, you're right. I'm from the Philippines.' She looks in the mirror and smoothens out her figure-hugging one-piece red dress.

'Aha. I thought you were from another country,' I respond as lightly as I can manage.

'There are many Filipinos working here, doing this kind job. We are cheap and popular with client. Cheaper than Korean girl but I'm first one at this place. I don't know why just me. Where you from? The States?'

'No, no, I'm from England.'

Play it cool. Gain her trust and don't lose her friendship.

'I never meet girl from England. I better go back, but nice meeting you.'

'Yes, chat later.'

She smiles and leaves. I finish off washing my hands and follow her shortly afterwards. Mi-Young is waiting for me at my table with a new client, who has already sat down. She stares coldly at me.

'Why you go toilet?' she hisses in my ear.

'Sorry, I really needed to go,' I tell her apologetically.

'You must entertain client. He waiting for you. We talk later.'

I nod my head and sit back down quickly. She walks away. I look over towards Francesca for a moment. She is sitting alone at her table, watching the events unfold at mine. She mouths something to me but I cannot make out what she is trying to say. I get back to singing songs for my client.

Something to ask her about later.

The clients all leave at the end of the night and the hostess girls all shuffle off together in their high heels. I notice Francesca is on her own again. Mi-Young and Mr Yi are both busy, trying to help a drunken client out of the bar and my captor is still nowhere to be seen. I bravely take the decision to chat to Francesca while all eyes are off us.

'Are you leaving now?' I ask.

'Yes, just need talk with Mi-Young. How about you?'

'I live here,' I say airily.

'Really? Why you live here?'

How should I answer this? I don't want to scare her off.

'I don't pay rent so it's cheaper for me.'

'Wow! You lucky girl!' she exclaims.

You don't know the half of it.

'It's good for me, yeah,' I agree, lying through my teeth.

Why did you say that? You idiot!

'Oh, what were you trying to say to me earlier?' I ask her, as if suddenly remembering.

'I said, "I'm bored".' She starts to laugh.

Mr Yi ushers the drunken client out of the club and locks the door while Mi-Young takes a glass that the client has been clutching back to the bar. She hasn't noticed us together yet.

Move away now before she sees us together.

'Okay, see you tomorrow, Francesca.'

'Yeah, see you.'

I put a little distance between us just before Mi-Young comes back to talk to Francesca.

Phew, I don't think she suspects a thing.

My captor walks in and speaks briefly to Mi-Young and Francesca, who both leave shortly after. He then turns his attention to me.

'Mi-Young say Mr Lee not come tonight. He still angry last night?' He sounds angry himself.

Unable to give him any answer to his question, I freeze in fear of what might happen next. He puts his hand around my throat and applies just enough pressure to make it hurt. I start to choke and try to release his grip with my fingers but he's way too strong for me.

'He important customer! I call him tomorrow. He come again, no problem.' He releases his grip and looks impassively at me as I wheeze uncontrollably, struggling for breath. Then he starts stroking my hair, almost lovingly, as though acknowledging he knows how important I am to him. 'If he don't come…' His face reddens and he stops stroking my hair. 'If he don't come then nobody care you here. You pray he come, understand?'

I nod my head in submission, still gasping for breath.

'Mr Yi, take her to room now,' he barks.

Chapter Fourteen

I'm sat at my usual place when Mi-Young comes to my table to escort yet another sorry state of a client to the door. He plonks a load of notes and coins in payment on the table and she smiles thinly, probably thinking that it's going to take her some time to count the money. She walks to the bar with him, moving out of sight behind a pillar. Meanwhile I glance at Francesca at the next table and see her getting up and heading towards the toilet. Mr Yi is busy welcoming customers at the main entrance so I make my move.

I arrive in the bathroom in time to see the back of Francesca, who is just going into one of the cubicles. I step into the other cubicle and wait for her to come out. My chance finally arrives so I take out my lipstick from my small bag, unravel some toilet roll and write a message on it.

Please help me. Charlotte.

I flush the toilet and leave the cubicle.

'Hi Francesca, are you well?' I ask her.

'Oh, hi. Good, thanks.' She's looking at herself in the mirror, applying some lipstick.

'Do you like working here?' I blurt out.

She stops what she's doing and looks at me. 'It's okay. You are friendly and sometimes we have chance speak but no-one else. Korean girl don't speak.' She returns to her work in the mirror. 'I speak a little Korean too so get angry that they don't speak to me.'

'Tell me about it. They haven't said a word to me.'

'Stupid girls. Always laughing.'

'Yeah, I couldn't agree more.'

We both laugh together.

She goes back into the cubicle, presumably in search of some more toilet roll. I notice that her partially open bag is sitting there between the taps on the wash basin.

Should I or shouldn't I? Oh, just put the bloody message in her bag. She's your only hope!

I pop it in and move away from the basin. A moment later the door opens and Mi-Young walks in, making me jump. My heart races as she's taken me by surprise, but I'm mightily relieved that she didn't walk in seconds earlier.

'Get back work now! Customer waiting. Mr Choi not happy. He no pay you do nothing!' she snaps heatedly.

Who is Mr Choi? It must be my captor! Finally I have a name.

Mi-Young advances on me, still fuming about catching me in here.

'Mr Lee come tonight. He very angry but now better. Don't anger him he never come back. He important customer. Last chance. Understand?'

'Yes, I understand.' I nod my head and she frogmarches me back into the bar. She points to my table and I get the message. Once I'm sitting down on my chair I see Francesca leaving the toilet, seemingly unnoticed by Mi-Young.

Minutes later Mi-Young arrives with a familiar face.

He's back then. Mr Choi will be happy, so at least he'll be off my back for a while.

Mi-Young glares at me as if to emphasize to me the importance of getting this evening right and back on track. I sense she wants me to apologise to Mr Lee.

'Mr Lee, I'm really sorry about the other night,' I say with sincerity.

'You make me angry but forget about it,' he replies. He looks into my eyes and his face mellows, seemingly enough for him to forgive and forget. He puts his hand on mine and looks at me adoringly, which is enough to convince Mi-Young that all is well again, so she turns

92

around and with a click of her heels glides back to the bar.

He gives my cheek a stroke. 'I thinking about you every day, all night. Think about you beauty, you voice. Please sing me song. It a long day today. So busy. I need soju.'

I suspect he's already been on the booze for a while as his breath stinks of alcohol and cigarettes.

I pour him a soju, which he knocks back immediately. He wipes his mouth with the back of his hand and gestures to me to pour him another one.

Oh God, this is going to be a long night.

'So why was today so busy?' I ask, while placing the microphone on the table.

'Many meeting all day.' He yawns, giving me the feeling that he wants to change the subject.

'Have you watched any baseball games recently?' I ask, choosing my topic carefully.

'Yes. LG beat rivals 7-1! I remember word,' he says, looking extremely pleased with himself.

'That's great. You must be over the moon!'

He frowns, puzzled. 'Why you say "over the moon", teacher?' he asks, leaning closer.

I hold in my breath so as not to breathe in his alcoholic fumes.

'It means really happy,' I tell him.

Unlike me right now!

He gives me a simpering smile. 'I see. You teach me well, sexy teacher.'

I feel his hand settle on my thigh.

'How about I sing another song?'

He nods his head.

Several songs and glasses of soju later he draws closer again and returns his hand to my thigh. He starts to massage my skin, which makes me cringe. Then he moves his hand up my leg, getting ever closer to my knickers, and mumbles things I don't understand in my

93

ear. He then kisses my cheek, gradually moving towards my mouth. I move my head slightly to ease him away from my lips without trying to make it obvious what I'm doing. I don't want him flaring up again. The smell of soju and stale cigarette smoke on him makes me want to retch.

Francesca, who has just finished with a client, looks across at me and sees my discomfort. She mouths something to me that I interpret as being 'you okay?' I nod my head so as not to let on that I'm in trouble in case anyone else might be looking my way.

Please, please look in your bag tonight and find my message!

His head suddenly slumps onto the table and I let out a huge sigh of relief.

Looks like the sojus have beaten him again tonight.

Mr Yi hurries over and it's not long before Mr Lee is on his way home.

Chapter Fifteen

'Charlotte, my beautiful, sweet daughter! Come here to me!' cries dad, who is clearly overjoyed to have me back home safely.

'I can't tell you how good it is to see you both right now!' I exclaim, hugging my parents across the airport barrier.

'Come here, Charlotte,' says mum as the three of us share a group hug. 'We'll meet you at the end of the line then we can sit down somewhere and have a coffee.'

As I walk along the barriers I see the journalists and paparazzi gathered together in a large group. All of a sudden I'm blinded by the flashes of the cameras as the paparazzi snap away, taking plenty of pictures of me. I draw closer to the journalists, who start firing their questions at me as soon as I'm within earshot.

'Did you do anything to lead Mr Lee on?' shouts one.

'Were you to blame for your own downfall?' yells another.

I look beyond the pack of wolves and catch my mum's disapproving face. She looks shocked at the questions the journalists are asking and whispers something to dad. Their joyful expressions have faded now and they look genuinely distressed at the thought of their sweet and innocent daughter maybe not being whiter than white.

While I'm still hemmed in by the reporters, mum grabs dad's hand and they head rapidly towards the airport exit, leaving me behind.

'Come back!' I plead, but my voice is drowned out by the questions of the press.

'Dad! Dad!'

I'm still screaming for him as I wake up from the nightmare and find myself still in my darkened cell, all alone.

I look around the bar from my table and spot the old man, who I entertained the other night.

A chance to do some more digging…

However, he is whisked away to another table and instead I am introduced to another new client, who is brought to my table. At least this one doesn't smell of stale cigarettes or strong alcohol.

Thank God for small mercies!

I find myself entertaining a younger man than most of the clients who frequent here. He's well-dressed but extremely shy and his English is elementary at best. He informs me that he's out with his boss and some of his work colleagues. He also tells me that word of mouth has got around about my being here and that this place is on the up again. He points to several of his colleagues around the club. Then he requests some songs, gazing into my eyes while I sing but keeping his hands to himself. Suddenly one of the men whom he had pointed at earlier rushes over and says something to him. The other man, who is much older than my client, taps his watch repeatedly. My client gets up from his seat and excuses himself, apologising profusely and assuring me he will come back soon, before they both dart out of the bar.

I don't have much time to think about what's just happened as my attention is drawn towards something more pressing as I see Francesca heading towards the toilet. I decide to take my chance to follow her in.

'Hi, Francesca,' I say as I dry my hands on a towel.

'Hi, Charlotte,' she replies in a low voice. 'I find your message in bag. We don't have time talk here. Mi-Young catch us big trouble. I write message back.' She produces a piece of paper. 'Take it, okay?'

'Thank you. I'll read it later.' I put the piece of paper in my bra.

The door is pushed open and my heart misses a beat. Fortunately it's just another hostess girl, who glances at me for a split second, then covers her mouth and laughs as though she were embarrassed. She hurries off to one of the cubicles, almost slipping over on the wet floor in her stilettos. She locks the door and I can still hear her tittering away to herself.

Mr Choi arrives at closing time and asks all the hostess girls to leave except Francesca and I.

Oh, shit! Does he know about the note?

He ushers us both into his small office, where Mi-Young and Mr Yi are already seated. Francesca and I sit down next to each other and exchange a brief glance. She looks as full of trepidation as I am.

Mr Choi stares hard at us. 'Mi-Young say you two always toilet together. Take time in toilet, she say.' He bangs his fist on the table. 'I want you work here, not there! Understand?'

Phew, at least he hasn't mentioned the note yet.

We both nod our heads and apologise.

'You two keep away. No talk any more!' He bangs his fist on the table again.

Francesca yelps with fright.

Well done, Charlotte. She ain't gonna help you now!

'Francesca go home,' Mr Choi orders.

She mutters her apologies as she grabs her handbag and leaves quickly, with Mr Yi in tow. Mi-Young gets up from her seat and, after bowing her head to Mr Choi, also leaves the room. Mr Choi gives them a good minute to leave the club, then suddenly turns my swivel chair around and pulls my head back, grabbing my hair. I cry out in pain.

'You cause me trouble!' he snarls. 'Mr Lee now Francesca!' His eyes are bloodshot and the smell of soju intensifies as he draws ever closer to me. 'No more you understand? No more!' He pulls my hair even harder, making me shriek. The tears start rolling down my cheeks. I try to loosen his grip but he slaps my face. 'I lose patience! Go to room now! Nobody make me stupid! Nobody!'

He releases me and I clutch my stinging cheek.

Mr Yi is called back to the office and is ordered to take me upstairs. I follow him obediently, still trembling and mortified from the abuse that I have just experienced.

Mr Yi pushes me into my cell, switching the light off on his way out. He locks the door and I am forced to grope my way to bed in near total darkness. I think about switching the light on myself in order to read Francesca's note, but worry in case he's waiting just outside. I find the bed and lie on it still fully clothed. I'm too tired to do anything more than kick my heels off.

Please help me, Francesca. You're my only hope.

Chapter Sixteen

The anticipation is killing me as I flatten out the scrunched-up piece of paper in the early morning light. Hoping that my problems are about to disappear, I eagerly read the message.

Why do you want my help? My job important to me. Make good money and too much risk. So sorry, Francesca.

I am stunned, though I don't blame her. It's not her fault after all. I am left in deep contemplation for a moment.

Why did I make that fucking phone call in the first place!

I try to think how I can somehow change Francesca's mind, but there seems no way to win her over. With nothing else to do, I try to go back to sleep, feeling like I'm going to be here forever.

Later on in the morning I'm awoken by the door opening. Mr Choi enters my room as I sit up.

He places a small plastic bag on the bed next to me. 'For face. You must to use. Remember, Mr Lee coming tonight.'

He contemplates me for a moment then turns on his heel and goes out, locking the door on his way out. I look inside the bag and find a small container. I examine it and see that it looks like skin foundation.

So that's it. He doesn't want Mr Lee to see the evidence of him slapping me.

Rebellion against the injustice of it all flares up in me so I decide to reply to Francesca's message in the hope that there's still a chance that all is not lost. Using my lipstick and a piece of toilet roll that I managed to sneak out from the club, I write her a second message.

Please help me get out of here. I need you. I've been kidnapped. Will you help me?

I fold up the piece of paper and put it in my pocket. All I need now is a way to give it to her without anyone suspecting anything.

That evening I get ready for yet another night at the hostess bar. I take the note out of my jeans and place it in my bra as I have nowhere else to put it. Just as I zip up the short, black dress I'm expected to wear the door opens and it's Mr Choi again standing there, this time accompanied by Mr Yi.

'No trouble tonight. No talk Francesca. Understand?' Mr Choi orders. His sidekick, Mr Yi, looks as menacing as ever, pounding one of his fists into the palm of his hand.

I nod my head and am led down to the club and instructed to take my usual seat and wait for the punters to arrive. I notice that Francesca is not at her usual table, so I scan the room and spot her strategically placed over the other side of the bar.

How am I going to get my message to her?

Just before the club opens, Mr Yi and Mi-Young bow to Mr Choi, who then disappears through the exit door.

It looks like he won't be around tonight. I wonder where he goes?

The bar opens and begins to fill up quickly with more clients filtering in than ever before. My heart sinks as I see Mi-Young approaching me with Mr Lee and a bottle of soju on a tray but she doesn't have time to stick around and spy on me, having to glide off to show other clients to their tables.

'Hello, Charlotte. I miss you,' he declares. He puts his jacket on the back of his chair and sits down. 'Wow! Very busy tonight. Philippine girl work here. Korean men like very much. Many people talk about her. She speak a little Korean too,' he says, clearly trying to make me feel jealous.

'Don't worry, my beloved,' he continues when he sees his taunt has had no effect, 'I prefer you... Maybe one day I teach you Korean.' He gives me a broad smile and lays his hand on mine. The thought of me being his beloved, makes my skin crawl.

'Would you like a drink?'

'You getting better,' he says as I fill his glass.

'What do you mean?'

'You no spill tonight.'

'Oh, I see.'

We both laugh, then he takes a swig.

'How does it taste?'

'Fine. Soju always same taste. You sing song for me tonight?' he enquires.

'Of course. I don't have the microphone so please excuse me.'

I can see that Mi-Young is busily showing clients to their seats so I go up to the bar in search of the microphone. I ask the bartender, who is looking stressed out due to all the clients propped up against the bar, if he has seen it but he cannot lay his hands on it, so he asks me to wait for a moment. I look to my left and there she is, Francesca, who's looking stunning in a blue sequined dress. She's waiting at the bar with two empty glasses. I look around to see if Mi-Young is close by but we are immersed in a sea of clients so I take my chance.

'Hiya,' I murmur as I sidle up next to her.

'What are you doing?' Francesca hisses back in alarm. 'Leave me alone!'

'I'm really sorry to have frightened you,' I mutter sincerely.

'Just go away. If they see us together we in trouble.'

She turns away from me but I notice that her small bag is open and, after a quick check that I'm not observed, I surreptitiously remove the piece of paper from inside my bra.

Now just put it in her bag!

I move closer to Francesca so that the bag is right under my elbow, then, with a last look around, I slip the note into it while she is still looking the other way.

'Microphone here, take!' says the disgruntled bartender, who is inundated with clients that have yet to be seated by Mi-Young. Everyone is waving money at him, wanting a drink. I hurriedly take the microphone from him and carry it and the remote control back to Mr Lee.

'Sorry for the wait,' I apologise, not wanting him to be upset any further.

'It's okay. Very busy tonight. Very busy.' He pats my thigh then runs his hand up towards the hem of my skirt.

Shit, he's not hanging about tonight. Do something!

I look at his glass and notice it's empty.

'Would you like another drink?'

He removes his hand from my thigh and holds his glass for me to pour him another. I try hard not to spill anything.

'My wife go some place with childrens,' he tells me. 'Can drink tonight. No problem!' His hand returns to my thigh.

Get your filthy paw off me!

'Sing song, please,' he requests.

As the evening wears on, my voice begins to show the strain of so much singing. I gulp down some water to keep going. Having knocked back the soju all night long, he is looking glassy-eyed but somehow manages to stay awake, though making less sense as the minutes pass by. Unfortunately I can see no sign of his eyelids starting to droop.

I don't think I can sing any more and sink back onto my chair. Once again, he places his hand on my thigh. This time he slides it slowly up between my legs, becoming more daring than ever before. He starts rubbing me in circular motions as he moves his head closer to mine.

'You like?' he whispers, breathing heavily and looking aroused.

I freeze, not quite sure what to say or do. My stomach is in knots and I feel like a panic attack is coming on. Everything inside me is shouting for him to stop but I just sit there, paralysed as his hands wander wherever he pleases. He starts rubbing me more vigorously, moving my satin panties aside, getting ever closer to my clitoris.

Trying to focus on something else, I notice that the heaving crowd of clients has dwindled somewhat. Mi-Young and the bartender are back in control again, leading clients to their tables and taking their orders. He removes his hand from my knickers just before Mi-Young walks past. He gestures her over to our table. They hold a muted conversation for a few seconds while I'm left to wonder what he's asking her.

Mi-Young nods her head and I fear for the worst when he hands over a wad of notes. She asks me to stand up, which I manage to do with some difficulty as my legs have started to tremble all over. I try to maintain my composure but sense the blood draining from my head, making me fear that I'm going to faint as we are led over to the dreaded burgundy curtains.

We go past the other hostess girls, who don't even look up, being too busy entertaining their own clients. I spot Francesca sitting nearby. She turns her head towards me but quickly looks away again when she sees Mi-Young and gets back to entertaining her client.

You're my only hope!

Mi-Young partially opens the curtains and shows us through. She closes the curtains again tightly behind us and I can almost sense her washing her hands of the whole sordid affair.

The red colour theme continues beyond the curtains. The walls and the sofa against one side are all a vivid red. He ignores the sofa, however, and pushes open one of a pair of doors on the opposite wall and leads me into

103

a further room, also done out in red, that I didn't even know existed previously. I find myself in a small space that is largely taken up by what appears to be a massage couch. While I'm still taking it all in, he grabs me by the waist and pushes me onto the couch. I find myself sliding around on the plastic cover.

'At last, we alone,' he mutters.

What can I do to distract him?

'More drink? I can get you one from the bar–'

'No time for drink!' he grunts as he hastily unbuttons his shirt. 'I pay many money tonight.' He takes off his shoes and in doing so almost falls over.

The soju's taking hold.

Now down to his pants he looks down at me, panting. 'Now you mine,' he sneers.

I try once more. 'Let me get you a drink. I'm sure you'd like–'

I start to get up off the couch but he pushes me back. 'Leave it! No time!'

He throws himself onto me and starts kissing my neck and mauling my breasts through my top. He reeks of soju, making me want to heave.

'Please,' I beg, 'I don't want this!'

'I no care what you want. I want you!'

'I'll scream!'

He just pauses and laughs, then slaps the wall with his hand. 'No one hear you!'

He tries to slip his hand up my skirt but my legs are crossed so his efforts are in vain.

'You play hard to get,' he mumbles as he carries on kissing my neck. 'I like but no time. Give yourself to me!'

'No!' I try to fend off his increasingly forceful assault on me.

Now he fastens his hand around my throat and starts squeezing until I'm struggling for breath.

'I pay for you. You do what I want!' he demands.

104

The squeezing intensifies and it's enough for me to give in to him. Imprisoned in this brothel of a red cage, I uncross my legs and allow him the freedom that he so desires. He releases his hold on my throat and drops his pants then pins me down on the couch. Holding my wrists out of the way with one hand, he uses the other to pull my knickers down to my ankles. Then he fumbles around for a condom from his wallet, quickly rips the packet open and slips it onto his penis. Breathing heavily with lust, he forces himself against me and I feel a piercing sensation as he starts moving inside me. I try to plead with him to stop but he ignores my protests. I try to take my mind off what he's doing to me, thinking about my family. I feel the tears begin to roll down my cheeks.

Within two minutes of the worst moment of my life, he's done as he reaches his climax. Afterwards he pulls his pants and trousers back up and chucks some notes on the couch, making me feel like some dirty whore.

'You good fuck,' he mutters. 'Buy something nice wear next time. We do again soon.' Then he slips out through the door without another word.

I tremble as I reach for my knickers and pull them back on. My eye falls upon the money he has left. Even though the sight of it makes me feel sick I grab it and thrust it down my top. It might prove useful to have money when I finally get out of here.

I wipe my tears dry and go back through the booth into the bar, walking a little unsteadily. Francesca looks towards me questioningly but averts her gaze again before I can communicate anything to her. I sit down gingerly at my table, praying that no other clients will come my way tonight. I barely have time to collect my thoughts, however, before I spot Mi-Young coming towards me with another customer. Without showing the least bit of concern or remorse, she instructs me to entertain the man and hands me the microphone. Feeling utterly miserable and hating her as much as I have ever hated anyone, I give her the ghost of a half-smile through gritted teeth before tapping in a song number.

When the night finally ends Mi-Young collects her belongings and leaves without speaking to me again. As soon as she's gone Mr Choi, who has reappeared towards the end of the evening, turns his attention to me. With only Mr Yi around, he strolls over and wraps an arm around me as he gives me a beaming smile.

'Private time good for you?' he enquires. I don't answer but he laughs out loud, then waves a substantial wad of notes in front of my face, depriving me of the last ounce of dignity I once had. 'Good for me! More private time for you in future!' He sniggers again, revealing his gold teeth, then goes off towards Mr Yi, who is sitting at the bar. I wait, standing numb and as unmoving as a statue, until they have finished their discussion and Mr Yi is ready to take me upstairs to my room.

Once more I'm pushed without ceremony into the cell and locked up for the night. When I look at my bed, however, I see a large bag lying on it. Inside I find a duvet and a pillow.

Do they think this makes up for what happened tonight? No, they are going to pay for this! I am going to make them pay! No more tears. Time to toughen up and get even.

Chapter Seventeen

I'm awoken by Mr Choi, who's sitting on the bed stroking my hair. I try to stay calm. There's a cooling breeze in the room rather than the normal sticky heat and when I look to see where it's coming from I see an expensive-looking air conditioner gently swivelling from side to side a few feet away.

'You sleep well?' His voice is unusually tender.

'Yes. Thanks.'

'You see. You do good thing for me I do good thing for you.' He points at the air conditioner.

I give him what I hope will pass for a smile. 'Thank you. It can get hot up here.'

God, it's difficult pretending to be grateful to him!

'You enjoy last night with Mr Lee?' The gold lumps appear one by one as his grin grows ever bigger, making me want to wipe that smile off his face. 'You cost me nothing but make me money. Good deal!' His smile now extends almost from ear to ear.

'I'm glad I make you happy. I want to make you lots of money,' I say, trying to sound genuine.

He laughs. 'Mr Lee come again tonight maybe, so this make me happy. It my lucky day when you come to me.' He lifts a bag up from the floor. 'I buy you new clothes. Here, take. Wear tonight, Mr Lee like.'

Don't show any reluctance.

He kisses me on my forehead, leans his head back and stares at me for a while. I sense some kind of change in his feelings towards me.

'You very beautiful.' He strokes my hair while licking his lips.

What's he thinking about now?

'Maybe blonde better than brunette.'

He moves in closer, getting ready to make his move, but I am saved by his mobile phone ringing. He takes it out of his pocket and looks at the screen. He mutters something that sounds unpleasant and then answers. He ends the call shortly after. I freeze.

'Very important. Go now.'

He leaves me my breakfast on a tray. At the door he turns back once more to admire his prized possession.

'Enjoy breakfast. Maybe next time,' he says cryptically.

Like I'm going to enjoy that shit, you bastard!

He goes out. I pick up the tray and examine it. There is a large bowl and a smaller one, both with lids on. I uncover the larger bowl, expecting to see the same old rice mush, but find instead what appears to be a healthy-looking soup. A meaty waft comes from it so I pick up a spoon and give the hot liquid a stir. My taste buds salivate as the flavours are released into the air. I see strips of beef, chopped onions and radishes and various green shoots, which I'm unable to identify.

I remove the lid from the smaller bowl, releasing steam from a mound of fluffy white rice. I wait a moment for it to cool down and then start hungrily on the two dishes. The taste is like no other, the spices setting off little explosions inside my mouth. Before I know it, I've emptied both bowls within minutes. I put the tray back on the floor, lick my lips and settle back on the bed, still savouring what I have eaten after days of completely tasteless meals.

That evening Mr Choi collects me from my bedroom and accompanies me downstairs to the bar. As I enter I notice that the place has been spruced up a bit. I detect an unpleasant smell as paint fumes begin to invade my nostrils.

'Take seat,' he says as we enter his office. He helps himself to a drink.

'Some problem tonight. I must to talk to you. Mr Yi is sick. Very sick.' He looks worried as he places his hand on his head and scratches it.

'I'm sorry to hear that. I hope he gets better soon,' I reply, though really I don't care if the man lives or dies.

'He no come tonight. I'm important business tonight so Mi-Young manage. Some problem, you must to speak her. I go soon.' He asks me to leave his office.

Shortly afterwards the club opens and the place starts filling up with clients. Thankfully there's no sign of Mr Lee. Mi-Young is busier than normal, rushing around trying to do two people's jobs, which gives me hope that I might get more freedom to move around unobserved.

My opportunity arises when Mi-Young heads off to the office and at the same time Francesca gets up from her chair to go to the toilet. Without any clients at my table, I get up and follow her in.

I enter the toilet and see that Francesca's applying some make-up at the basin. My heart pounds as I debate what's best to do.

'Hi, Francesca,' I greet her nervously.

'Hi, Charlotte. I see your note,' she murmurs.

'And?'

'Mr Choi is danger if you say true. I don't know if I…' She puts her make-up away in her bag but I can tell she's wavering.

'Look, I know it's a difficult decision but please believe me. I'm telling you the truth. One hundred per cent. Please help me. I'm begging you for your help!' I start to tremble all over as I give it everything I've got.

Francesca looks away from me. 'I'm sorry. I have to go. I cannot help you. We shouldn't talk.' She takes a step towards the door.

'He raped me!' I collapse onto the floor in a state of shock, unable to see clearly through the tears that are welling up.

Please come back!

'Rape? What? Who raped you?'

I can just make out through the tears that she's turned back to me. She picks me up from off the floor, checks that there's nobody else around, then guides me into one of the cubicles and closes the door behind us.

'Okay. I help,' she says, suddenly changing her mind. 'We can talk here but quiet. Tell me what happen.' Her concern for me is etched on her face.

'My client did, last night. He took me into a room through the booths at the back and raped me. You saw me, didn't you?'

Francesca's mouth drops open. 'But they say it's just massage room – no more.' She looks outraged. 'He said me! I can't believe! I hate him! Come here, poor girl.' She puts an arm around my shoulder and tries to comfort me, taking some toilet roll and drying my eyes.

'It's true, it's true,' I sob. 'He took me in there and raped me and Mr Choi let it happen because *he* was given money! You have to believe me!'

'Shh! Too loud,' Francesca warns me. 'My God!' She looks shocked. 'Massage okay. It's normal, but this no. No good.' She pauses to take a deep breath. 'I want help you but we think smart. Don't talk, look at each other. Be nice to Mr Choi. Make him like you.'

'Yes, I understand.' I wipe my face, feeling relieved that I finally have someone on my side. 'I'm already doing that.'

'Mr Yi is no here. Maybe long time no coming but I don't know. We have more chance to leave. I write a plan and give to you tomorrow. Try to come here at nine before it too busy,' she says quickly.

The main door to the ladies toilet opens and we both freeze. I try to work out how many people have come in as we listen to the clicking of heels across the floor and loud chatter. Francesca takes a peek under the door and puts two fingers up to indicate the number of people she can see. The girls are giggling to themselves about something. The door opens again and the bathroom goes quiet so Francesca points to me to hide behind the cubicle door, then flushes the toilet. She opens the door gently and leaves. I hear the main door open and close again a moment later but can still hear someone's voice so decide to wait a little longer. The door opens and closes again and then the room goes silent so I take my chance and edge out of the cubicle, hoping for the best. I check the mirror to smarten myself up and apply some fresh make-up before leaving.

Everything looks calm in the club so I make my way back to my table, sit back down and scan the room for Mi-Young.

Phew! She must still be in the office.

Francesca is close by, busily entertaining a client. I quickly run through what she has told me to do. I also consider how to deal with Mr Lee if he arrives on the scene.

Halfway through the evening Mi-Young, who is looking mightily tired by now, brings the nasty little excuse for a man to my table, along with his drink. Not wanting to displease him, I stand up to greet him. Mi-Young fixes her steely eyes on me and tells me to look after my guest before rushing off, rather less poised than usual, to deal with other clients, who are waiting at the bar to be seated.

Mr Lee takes off his jacket and I put it on the back of his chair for him. Once seated next to me, he grabs my hand.

'I miss you,' he tells me.

I give him a smile. 'I've missed you, too.'

I'm going to have your balls served up on a plate! And Mr Choi's too!

'Yesterday so special for me. I wish longer time so sorry.'

You fucking wanker! I'm going to make you suffer!

'Yes, me too. What shall I sing for you tonight?'

111

'Aww, Beatles.'

THE Beatles, you asshole! Can't you think of any other bloody band!

'The Beatles it is. Bear with me for a moment. I'll just go and get the microphone.'

He nods his head, then pats my bottom as I squeeze past him.

Get off me!

I pass by Francesca on my way to the bar but she doesn't look up. Mi-Young is fanning herself to keep cool.

'Why you here? You should go to client,' she barks at me.

'I need the microphone and the machine.'

She scowls. 'Okay. I get it.' She looks harassed and haggard.

I hope Mr Yi's off work for a long time. The more tired she gets the more mistakes she'll make…

Mi-Young hands the equipment to me and tells me to get back to work. I walk back to the table and search for Mr Lee's favourite song on the machine.

When the song ends he grins. 'You sing good tonight. Sing another.' He places his hand on my thigh and starts stroking it.

Don't let him see how much he disgusts you. Stay calm. Try to get him drunk.

'More soju?' I ask.

'Yes. Today very busy.' He takes his hand off my thigh and gulps down a whole glassful of the liquid.

Keep his glass full all night. He's bound to fall asleep sooner rather than later.

'So why was today busy?' I enquire.

'Too much customer.' He shakes his head. 'I don't want talk about job. I want relax with you.'

'Yes, that's a good idea.' I look at him and wink as I hand him another glassful.

Drink up!

112

He swigs it down.

'You just sit there, drink and relax while I sing you another song.'

'Charlotte, you great girl. You make me happy.' He starts rubbing his crotch.

I try to focus on something else. I notice one of the other hostess girls leading a client towards the burgundy curtains.

Just a massage or added extras?

Reality hits once again as he moves his hand too far up. I remove it and place it back on his knee.

'Maybe later, Mr Lee, if you are a good boy,' I tell him, winking suggestively.

As if!

'You play with me. I like it,' he replies. He picks up his glass and takes another big gulp.

My plan works exactly as intended. By the time the club is at its busiest later that evening, he is slurring his words and can barely keep his eyes open.

'I go now. Feel sleepy.'

Yes!

He attempts to get up but stumbles. Mi-Young, who is busy entertaining another client close by, comes over to assist him in leaving the club. They get halfway to the doors when Mr Lee stumbles again, taking Mi-Young and a table full of drinks down with him. A hostess girl and her client, who are sitting at the table narrowly avoid getting soaked, moving their chairs back just in time.

The place goes quiet and for the first time since I have been here, I hear concern from the hostess girls. The two closest girls rush over to assist. Mi-Young gets up slowly and cries in pain. I move a little closer and see that she has a gash on her head. She rushes off to the toilet to clean herself up, directing the girls to look after Mr Lee.

Mr Lee, who is oblivious of the chaos that he has caused, is helped up by the two girls and doesn't appear

113

to have any cuts or injuries. He scratches his head and points to something, which I can only assume is the door, but he's miles off course. The two girls escort him out of the building, along with some of the other clients, who have perhaps had enough of the evening's events.

One of the hostess girls returns to her client. The other hurries to the toilet, presumably to look after Mi-Young. The barman deals with the broken glass and spillages.

I glance towards Francesca's table and see that she's without a client.

A chance! I just need to get her attention.

I wait to see what happens. Mi-Young, who's holding her hand to her head, and the hostess girl emerge from the toilets and head straight into the office. I pick up the glasses from my table and walk past Francesca, mouthing 'toilet now' to her and discreetly pointing her in the right direction. I put the glasses down at the bar and head towards the ladies. She follows me in a few moments later.

'Cubicle?' I suggest as she joins me at the basin. She nods her head.

I lock the door behind us. 'I think we have to go now. It's our best chance,' I whisper.

She looks alarmed. 'I'm not sure…'

'No, no. Now is our best chance,' I insist. 'Nobody will pay attention to us. Let's just make a run for it together. I reckon we have about ten minutes before Mi-Young will be back.'

'I don't know…'

'Please!' I beg. 'You have to come with me. I don't know this city. I've never ventured out of this place before.' I throw in my clincher. 'This place. It isn't safe for *you* either. They'll know it was you who helped me.'

The expression on Francesca's face changes. She looks frightened now, perhaps realising to what extent she's up to her neck in all this. I sense she might cave in.

'Okay, okay, I come with you,' she agrees finally.

114

'Thank you, Francesca! This means so much to me. I promise there's a better future waiting for you than this.'

'Okay,' Francesca instructs me. 'I go first and we walk out of the bar slowly. First me, then you. I wait for you outside. Around corner. Turn left when you come out of building. Wait one minute here then come. Meet you outside.'

Francesca opens the toilet door, checks that it's clear, looks back and wishes me 'good luck' and then goes. I begin the count in my head. My heart beats faster as I do my best not to jumble up the numbers.

...fifty-nine, sixty. Go!

I open the bathroom door and walk out as if nothing strange is going on. I walk around the edge of the hostess bar. Nobody seems to notice me at all and I cannot see Mi-Young anywhere. Through the slightly open office door I catch a glimpse of her still being treated by the hostess girl.

She's too busy caught up with her own problems to be noticing me.

I approach the main doors. The barman is busily putting the table back on its legs and tidying up.

Nobody to stop you now.

I open the main door and slip out undetected.

I've made it!

My eyes take a moment to adjust to the darkness outside. I head off up the deserted street, turn left and spot Francesca standing next to a street light. She waves at me so I take off my high heels and run towards her.

'We did it!' I exclaim.

'Ssh! Quiet! We are no free yet. We walk to next street and get taxi. I book one when waiting for you,' she tells me.

'I have some money we can use,' I reply, referring to the tip Mr Lee threw on the massage couch.

'That's great. We go to hotel far away from here. Not my home because he know my address.' She looks down

115

at my feet. 'Put heels back on. Look normal,' she advises.

We quicken our pace, both of us desperate to get to our taxi. A car comes our way, its headlights blinding us. It goes past but then I hear the distinct sound of it reversing.

'It's him!' Francesca shouts. 'Run!'

We take off our heels and race down the street. Behind us we hear a car door open and shut. The chase is on as we hear footsteps pounding in hot pursuit. In the distance I can see the lights of a much busier-looking road. Freedom is so tantalisingly close that I can almost feel it.

'Just get to that street!' Francesca gasps.

The footsteps behind us are getting louder so we are forced to change our plan and turn left down a narrow, dimly lit side-street in an attempt to lose our pursuer. Seeing that we are running towards a dead end, however, Francesca grabs my arm and points at some large industrial bins close by. We make our way behind one of them and crouch down. The putrid smell coming from inside the bin makes me want to throw up but I try to control my breathing as silence descends around us. A trickle of sweat runs down my forehead. We listen for the footsteps but hear nothing. I look at Francesca but she just looks blankly back at me, shrugging her shoulders.

Moments later we hear the footsteps again, this time getting very close. I start to panic and fear that the game could be up.

'I know you here. Come to me now, I no hurt you.' We both recognise Mr Choi's voice. We stay rooted where we are, having nowhere else to go.

A ringing tone suddenly goes off next to me. I stare in horror at Francesca, who is frantically trying to turn off her mobile phone.

'Come out, I know you here,' Mr Choi yells.

116

I turn to Francesca.

'Run!' she mouths.

We both get up and make a dash for it. We make it back to the road that we were previously on and turn left in the direction of the bright lights.

I glance behind and see *him* just a few feet behind us.

'I'm sorry, Francesca!' I gasp.

A hand grabs my dress. Then I see a gloved hand seize Francesca's shoulder. We are both pulled back and shoved against a wall. The bright lights of the distant street seem a million miles away as we find ourselves staring wide-eyed and panting up at our tormentor.

'Smart but not that smart. You see?' Mr Choi gestures with his hand. 'Nobody round here. Just old factory, no house, no shop. No-one here to help.' He laughs like a hyena that has just outwitted its prey.

We are forced to walk in front of him back the way we came. He keeps a firm hold of both of us until we reach his car, which is parked at an angle across the street.

'Get in!' he orders.

He hits Francesca hard on the back of her neck as she gets in and she slumps onto the back seat.

'Push her over,' he instructs me.

I bend down to shove Francesca over to the other side of the vehicle.

'Now you in!'

I am just getting into the car myself when he hits me.

Chapter Eighteen

'What's going on?' I mumble, trying to adjust my eyes to the dimly lit surroundings that I've woken up in. I try to wipe my mouth but realise that my hands are tied behind my back.

I manage to lift my head up to look around. The first thing I see is Francesca, gagged and tied to a chair. She's so close to me that I could touch her if my hands were not tied. Her head is bowed but I can see that her face is cut and blood is dripping from her nose onto her bloodstained skirt.

'Francesca! What has he done to you?'

All of a sudden I feel hands going around my neck and tightening their grip like a python constricting the breath out of its prey.

'To think I like you before!' he whispers in my ear. 'You try make me look stupid? See what you do?' he screams at me from behind. 'You do this! This position we in. This *you* fault! You try escape from me. Big mistake!'

His hands get tighter still. Then he lets go and moves around so that he can stare me in the face. He looks about ready to explode.

'You important for me but Francesca, no problem. Can find other girl. She no have family. Live on street in Philippine. Come here for better life. Nobody care.' He switches his gaze to Francesca. 'Such a pretty girl. Now look! You do this!' He punches her in the face, and I hear a small whimper from behind the gag. The blood from her nose runs faster than before.

'Please, let her go!' I beg. 'It's me you want, not her.'

Mr Choi turns back to me and grabs me by the throat again. He raises his hand and I fear for the worst, but then he laughs like he's deranged and batters Francesca once more instead. The whimper she gives is softer than before and I begin to fear for her life. Her chin is covered with blood.

He unties the gag and lifts up her face. 'What you say?' Amused by her lack of response, he laughs again like the devil possessed. 'She no good me. Who want "beautiful" woman like this?'

'Please, Mr Choi,' I plead. 'Don't kill her!'

He glares at me. 'How you know my name?'

His vice-like grip goes back around my throat and I begin to choke.

Oh, shit!

'Tell me how you know my name?' he repeats. '*She* tell you?' His hand clenches into a fist.

'No, no, it wasn't her,' I croak. 'Please believe me!'

'Who? Tell me!'

He applies more pressure and my head starts to spin.

'It was Mi-Young. She told me by mistake,' I splutter.

'Why she do this? Stupid woman!'

He's still squeezing and I'm close to losing consciousness but then he lets go and I gasp for air. While I recover, he puts on a pair of black gloves, slowly as if to prolong my agony. Then he takes out a gun and waves it around like a madman.

'Somebody pay for mistake!' he yells.

'Please don't touch her. Let her go!'

'Let her go? Impossible!'

He turns and punches Francesca in the face yet again. A tooth flies out of her mouth and a pool of blood has formed on the floor. There's no sound from her this time and I fear the worst.

'She ugly and stupid. I no want her. You fault she here. You live with this day for you life.'

He stands by her side and points the gun at her head. 'She have no life now. Before she have life. My bar. I pay her. Good job. Her life ruin. Not me! Now you watch her die!'

119

His finger tightens on the trigger. Unable to watch, I close my eyes.

'Please don't do it! Kill me instead!'

'You do this – no me! I kill her because *you* mistake!'

Then he fires. The sound is so loud it reverberates inside my head for what seems forever. I feel dizzy. I keep my eyes closed when I feel the muzzle of the gun prodding my temple.

'Finish. Now you do everything I say! Open eyes now! No time for game.'

I open them slowly and see that he's standing in front of me with a handkerchief covering his mouth, pointing his gun at me. His bloodshot eyes make him look the epitome of all things evil.

'Put her in this.' He gestures with the gun at some kind of bag lying on the floor at his feet. I've seen bags like it before, but only on the television news. It's a body bag.

I nod my head to show I will cooperate. Then I glance at Francesca, still slumped in the chair.

Oh my God! What have I done to you?

My stomach muscles tighten as I feel the urge to throw up but there's nothing left inside me. I try to turn away but everywhere I look I see bits of her brains and blood splattered all over the place. A pool of her blood is slowly spreading across the floor towards me, just inches from my feet.

Mr Choi unties my hands and kicks the body bag towards me.

'Okay, put her in bag now!'

Shaking all over I get up off the chair and lean over Francesca's battered body to untie her hands and legs. Mr Choi keeps the gun trained on me as I unzip the body bag. The zip gets stuck and he shouts at me to hurry up. My trembling hands yank at the zip and it gets caught again.

'Quick!' he screams at me, losing his temper. He prods the gun against my temple again.

'Why don't you just kill me and do the job yourself?' I cry out, my voice quivering.

'Silence!' He taps my temple gently with the gun.

After much fumbling, I eventually get the bag open and lay it out flat on the floor. Then I grab Francesca around the waist and haul her down onto it. Now on my hands and knees and trying not to look at her mangled face, I pull the flaps up and slowly begin to zip the bag back up, avoiding getting it caught.

I'm so sorry it ended like this, Francesca.

With the bag now zipped up, he beckons me over. With wobbly legs, I follow him out of the small room, where Francesca lies and he leads me down a narrow corridor to a bathroom.

'Clean up,' he orders. 'Take off clothes. Put in bag and have shower. Be quick!'

I remove my bloodstained clothes and place them in a bin bag that he's holding out to me. I notice that his own clothes have remained completely clean.

It should be you who has blood on your hands!

I stand there naked in front of him. He surveys me admiringly. 'You have beautiful body. I can see why Mr Lee love you. I prefer brunette,' he reaffirms. 'Like you friend in England. Maybe she visit one day.'

How can you think of that at a time like this? You're one sick son of a bitch!

I get in the shower and turn it on. The icy cold water makes me shiver. I back away but he waves me under the shower head with his gun. I look down and see a river of blood draining away down the plug hole, making me feel queasy. A couple of minutes later, the water runs clear again.

'You clean?'

I nod my head. He hands me a towel and points at a pile of clothes on a chair in the corner.

121

'Be quick. We go soon.'

I wrap the towel around me and step out of the shower. He keeps the gun pointed at me while I dry myself and get dressed.

'You look beautiful again.'

He comes up to me and strokes my hair with his gloved hands. I remain entirely silent, waiting for him to stop. He seems to sense my hostility and takes a step back.

'We put body in car and take it to special place where cannot ever find,' he tells me. 'Make no mistake, you play trick again, you be next.'

We go back to the other room. He orders me to drag Francesca's body to the door. Once the bag's in the corridor he closes the door and locks it. Then he walks behind me, pointing the gun at my back while I drag the bag down the corridor. I struggle to keep the bag moving.

'I can't do this any more!' I gasp as the body bag slips from my hands for the umpteenth time.

'Pick her up and do job!' he demands, prodding his gun in my back.

I summon up every last ounce of energy I have and pull the bag further down the passageway.

We reach another door, which he instructs me to open. I drag the body bag through it and he turns on the light to reveal we are in a large garage, standing between two expensive-looking cars. He opens the boot of one of them.

'Put her in and get in front.'

I struggle to lift the bag into the boot by myself so he reluctantly helps me. Then he slams the boot shut and motions me into the car before getting in himself, still wearing his gloves. As he starts up the engine I glance at the clock, which reads three-ten a.m. The garage door opens and we drive smoothly out. I notice the automatic door close again in the mirror as we drive up a long, steep slope. Thirty seconds later we reach a pair of large gates that open automatically as we approach them. Once the gate has fully opened we drive out onto the open road.

He waits for a moment to check that the gate has closed behind us. It's pitch black out here and there's not a trace of life around as we drive along a bumpy single-track road. Each bump makes my already sick stomach churn some more as I struggle to comprehend what has happened this sorry night.

'That house like Fort Knox. Same same! Nobody get in there,' he boasts, laughing out loud.

One of these days I'm going to ram that laugh of yours up where the sun doesn't shine.

The car's headlights briefly light up a signpost as he prepares to turn off the single-track road. I try my best to read it but the bumpiness of the road and the sign's reflectiveness make it nigh on impossible. Things then get even bumpier as we probe through the undergrowth on a track of dried mud and grass, relying on the headlights to guide us. A sudden drop in elevation nearly causes Mr Choi to lose control. He battles with the steering wheel to stop the vehicle ending up in a bush.

'We here,' he says triumphantly about five minutes after turning off the single-track road.

Just before he switches off the engine I glance at the clock, which reads three-forty-two a.m.

He gets out of the car and walks round to my side, where he taps on the window and signals me to get out too. Once I'm out he points the gun at me and orders me around to the back of the car.

The night is sticky and my skin is moist with sweat. The moon appears from behind a cloud and I take the opportunity to establish what I can of our surroundings. Despite it being dark I can see that there appears to be only the one track leading in and out of the area.

123

He tells me to pick up the bag and drag it along with me. He walks just in front of me, the gun always trained in my direction. Using the light on his mobile phone for guidance, he leads me down a narrow, overgrown path until we reach a wide open space with a path that leads both ways. Utterly exhausted, I drop the body bag on the ground and look around.

The full moon reveals another signpost, directly in front of me, but it's too dark to read what it says. I also see the shine of the moon being reflected off a large body of water in the distance. I look to my left and make out the outline of a dimly lit, ornate-looking building not too far away. It would appear that the path we are standing on winds its way down to that very same building.

Could be some kind of tourist destination maybe?

He realises I've halted. 'Why you stop? Take body now!'

'I can't!' I exclaim. 'Look at me – just look at me!'

'No time now!' he says aggressively. He takes up a shooting stance and points the gun at my head. 'Take body now!' he repeats.

I remain where I am, defying him.

'You leave me no choice!' he snaps. He lowers the gun and produces a pair of handcuffs from his pocket. He cuffs me and puts the key back in his pocket, then picks up the body at the head end and starts dragging it along the ground with one hand, still pointing his gun at me with the other and grumbling away in Korean all the way.

He leads me off the path and down another overgrown track, using the moon's light for guidance. After a few minutes he suddenly stops. I can see that we've come out at the top of a steep drop over the edge of the lake. The moonlight briefly disappears and then reappears again, glistening on the surface of the tranquil water for a moment before it disappears behind yet another cloud.

'This lake one of the deepest in Korea,' he informs me. 'Much people don't come here. Some say bad thing happen here. You disappear, nobody look for you here.'

He points the gun at my head again and tells me to open the bag. I bend down and fumble around trying to find the zip. Eventually I manage to unzip it.

He gestures at the ground around us. 'Plenty of big rock here. Put them in bag now!'

'You're crazy!' I burst out.

Did I really just say that?

'Maybe yes! Clever crazy!' He laughs again, confirming my already strong conviction that I'm dealing with a murderous megalomaniac.

I feel around in the dark for suitable rocks.

'This is too difficult with these handcuffs on,' I complain. 'Please can you take them off?'

He begrudgingly removes the cuffs and orders me to hurry up. My arms ache as I heap dozens of stones into the bag containing Francesca's body.

'Hurry! No time. More rock!' he shouts at me whenever I pause for breath.

When the bag's nearly full, he hands me something wrapped in a bin bag and tells me to put it inside as well. I take it from him and notice that it's the same bag that I put my dirty clothes in earlier. He directs the light from his mobile phone at the body bag so I can see what I'm doing. I zip the body bag up with some difficulty as the zip catches and I notice that my hands are slippery with blood once more.

'Okay,' Mr Choi demands. 'Push body over now!'

With great difficulty I drag the bag right up to the edge of the drop.

'Please, don't do this,' I plead, gasping for breath. 'You'll never get away with it!'

He bends down and whispers in my ear. 'You forget, she don't have family! Now she join Chris in lake!'

Chris? No!

'No – you join him!'

Risking my worthless life, I take a swipe at him to try and push him over the edge, but it's a pitiful attempt as he barely moves an inch, though the surprise attack does make him drop his phone, which falls into the lake.

'Why you do that?' he rages at me. 'You stupid bitch!'

He slaps me across the face, making me yelp. Then he points his gun at my head.

'Do it now!' he orders icily.

Mustering all of my energy I push the body over the edge. Seconds later I hear a loud splash as it hits the surface of the water and begins to sink.

He hauls me up onto my feet and sticks the gun in my back. 'Finish. Now we go.'

Feeling dizzy and lightheaded, I walk ahead of him back to the car. My mind is whirling like an out-of-control washing machine on maximum setting. It's all too much for me to cope with – murder, disposing of a body in a lake – and on top of all that being told that Chris's body is also somewhere in there.

We arrive back at the car. He pushes me in and locks the door then clambers into the driver's seat.

'You tell anyone, I kill you just like Tatiana,' he warns me as he turns the key in the ignition. 'So keep mouth close.'

Who the fuck is Tatiana? Is that the Russian girl the old man was talking about?

His gold lumps appear one by one as he knows he's got the better of me. 'No trust any more. Wear these.' He forces the pair of handcuffs back on me and returns the key in his pocket.

As he starts to drive off, my eyes settle on the car's clock, which reads four-oh-seven a.m. He takes us back along the same hazardous excuse for a road that we drove in on, but this time going with more care after our close call on the outward journey.

126

A road sign lights up briefly as we reach the junction that leads us back onto the single-track road. It says something in Korean that I cannot read, but written below is the word 'Danger' in English. We turn off down the road and I try to remember anything else that will help me identify the spot later on. The road eventually improves but I'm unable to spot anything noteworthy that tells me where we are. I look at the time again. It is four twenty-eight a.m. as we finally reach a main road. The signpost reads 78, which I can only assume to be the road number. Seoul is signposted to the right, with a place named Sinsan-Ri to the left. As I expect, we turn right towards the city.

'Wake up! Wake up!'

I stir from my sleep that's overtaken me and see that we are driving into a small underground car park. The clock tells me it has just turned five twenty a.m. We get out of the car and enter the building above via a narrow stairwell. Various tell-tale signs tell me that we are back at his apartment block near the club. We ascend to my cell and he unlocks the door, turns the light on and pushes me in. I expect him to lock the door and leave, but instead he grabs my arm and throws me onto the bed. The next moment he is on top of me.

I try to wriggle free but he pins me down.

'See what happen when try fuck with me?' he hisses.

I go very still until he is satisfied that he has made his point and heaves himself off me. He removes my handcuffs, gives me a last glare, and then turns the light off and locks the door behind him, leaving me alone.

I grope for the photo that Rachel gave me and hold it tight, even though I can't see her in the dark. I curl up into a ball, unable to close my eyes, and stare into the darkness around me.

Oh, Rach. They must be looking for me by now, right? Think of me. I need your strength to help me through this...

127

Chapter Nineteen

The doors suddenly burst open, flattening Mr Yi, who is standing beside them. I recognise the intruder's face straightaway.

'Joe!' I jump out of my seat as he marches over towards Mr Choi.

'Oi! You're gonna fucking pay for this!'

'Joe, no! You don't know what he's like!' I shrill.

Joe grabs hold of Mr Choi and starts pummelling his fist into his face.

As I start to open my eyes to the morning light it dawns on me that I am not alone.

'Joe,' I mutter, still half asleep, 'is that you?'

'Who you talk about?'

It's Mr Choi's voice. My eyes snap open as he grabs my hair and pulls me up from the mattress. 'Who is Joe?'

'Joe is nobody. I hate him!' I stammer.

Almost as much as I hate you!

'Why you call he name?' he barks, twisting my hair in his hands. 'He live here Korea? You contact him?'

'No, no, he doesn't live here. He was my ex-boyfriend in the UK but he's nobody to me,' I explain quickly, trying to calm him down.

'No understand. Why you say he name?'

'I don't want to talk about him.'

'Tell me!'

He jerks my head back, making me cry out with pain.

I think back to what Joe did to me and sparks begin to fly around inside my head. 'You remember the scar?'

He looks confused so I point to it on my arm and then he twigs.

'He did that to me. He was trying to rape me and threw me onto the floor. He broke my arm!'

He releases my hair. 'He sound like strong man. Maybe he could work my club!' He emits a bellow of laughter.

'Do you have no compassion?' I say softly, smoothing my hair down.

He looks perplexed, perhaps not understanding my question. Still with a baffled look on his face, he decides to change the subject.

'Last night – wow!' He grins at me like he's a hunter boasting of some kind of trophy killing. Then he looks stern again. 'You see my power. Yesterday our secret, yes?'

I nod my head in fear. He leans forward and kisses me on the cheek like an indulgent uncle.

Murderer! You are going to pay for this!

He turns his attention to the plastic bag he has brought with him as well as my breakfast. 'I buy this for you. Perfect for you, Mr Lee favourite colour.' He holds my face in both his hands, 'Wear dress tonight for him.'

Mercenary, pimping bastard!

He rises, but before he leaves the room he flashes me a devilish smile and whips the duvet and pillow from my bed and tosses them through the door. Then he unplugs the air conditioner and takes that too, just to torture me further.

'Forget Joe,' he advises me. 'You have someone else who like you.'

He gives another thundering laugh as he finally goes, locking the door from the other side.

I digest what has just been said and then pick up the tray to see what he has left me. This time there are no lids and no steam wafting in my face, only bland, cold food and a bowl of rice. I sigh as I realise he has decided to deny me what little comfort I had.

Later on he comes to supervise me while I shower and change and then takes me down to the club.

129

'Ahh, you look beautiful in dress. Mr Lee will like. Come,' he says when I'm ready.

The hostess girls arrive a bit earlier than usual this evening and with Mr Choi unexpectedly hanging around the club I sense that some kind of announcement is going to be made. As I expect, within a minute or so he calls them over for a meeting. I appear to be excluded.

As if anyone gives a toss about me anyway.

Mr Yi is also absent, which leads me to think that this might be another cause for the meeting. Before launching into proceedings, he pauses and looks at me then seems to indicate to the others that they must wait for a moment. He strides over to me at my table and instructs me to clean some glasses at the bar.

Could this be more punishment?

Then he walks back over to the girls and begins the meeting, hollering at them in a loud, overbearing voice. Everything is in Korean, but I hear Francesca's name being mentioned on more than one occasion – but that's all I can glean from his rant.

I wish I knew what he was saying.

The girls remain impassive, which doesn't give me any hint about what might be being said about their missing colleague, but then again I don't expect much sign of emotion from those airheads. The only thing that seems to get them going is when a nail gets broken or mascara smudged.

After the meeting has finished it is business as usual and we're instructed to wait for our clients at our usual tables. Mr Choi approaches me with Mi-Young, who has covered up her cut from the previous night with plenty of foundation cream.

Oh, my God! If looks could kill!

He suddenly notices something amiss elsewhere in the room and apparently orders Mi-Young to sort things out. She bows her head and rushes off majestically to deal with whatever the problem is. Once she's gone he leans over me.

'Mr Yi sick again so I stay here tonight. Watch you all night,' he says menacingly. 'So sad that Francesca go back to Philippines. But she want to see family.'

It suddenly dawns on me what he's told them.

My mind goes back to last night. 'But you said she doesn't have any family,' I remind him.

He sticks his face right in front of mine. 'I know that and you know that. How you tell them? You no speak Korean and they no speak English. So our secret, yes?' The lumps that I hate so much reappear.

I expect those dizzies believe every bloody word.

After he has walked away, Mi-Young reappears with a spray cleaner in her hand and a menacing look on her face.

'You get me into trouble again and you life not worth living!' she says venomously.

'It isn't worth living anyway,' I retort. I decide to show my hand. 'Do you really want to know what happened to Francesca? Because I can tell you.'

She scowls at me. 'Don't make up story. She come back home, just like Mr Choi say. Mr Choi always say the truth.'

'If that's what you want to believe then so be it, but it simply isn't true!' I tell her stubbornly.

'*You* lie!' she snarls. 'I watch you *every* move.' She glares at me for what seems like an eternity, trying to strike fear into me.

I shrug. 'You believe what you like. I don't bloody well care any more.'

Before she can respond, Mr Choi, who's now over on the far side of the club, shouts orders at her and she rushes off.

Yes sir, yes sir, three bags full sir.

When the bar opens a few minutes later Mr Choi takes on Mr Yi's role, opening the door and bowing his head to all the great and good who walk through it. One of the first to arrive is Mr Lee. He engages Mr Choi in deep conversation and I catch a glimpse of him handing over an envelope.

I wonder what that's about?

Then it's Mi-Young's turn to greet Mr Lee. He says something to her and hands her a gift-wrapped present.

Maybe some sort of apology for his behaviour last night?

Mi-Young bows her head in thanks and walks him to my table. He then turns his attention to me.

'Wow. Beautiful dress. My favourite colour. Look like Marilyn Monroe,' he says as Mi-Young stalks off with his jacket hanging over her arm.

We both sit down and Mi-Young brings the drinks over to us. She looks at me coldly, giving me the feeling that she's still smarting about being scolded by Mr Choi before leaving us alone.

'Last night too much drink,' Mr Lee remarks.

'You drank a lot, yes.'

But not enough, because you've made it here today!

'Maybe I don't drink so much tonight. Headache all day.'

I'm in charge of your drinks so don't count on it…

'So how are you?' he asks.

Rape, murder and mad owner. I feel on top of the world, you prick!

'Yes, I'm well.' I pour him a drink. 'Have you watched the Twins recently?'

'No game since last time I come,' he replies. He takes a swig of his drink.

'Are there any other sports you like?'

'Football is so so but don't watch many time. Baseball is best game.'

I feel that I'm running into a sporting dead-end.

'So when are the Twins next playing?' I ask, clutching at straws.

'Next game away so no go,' he says rather glumly.

The night goes by slowly as Mr Lee requests song after song. Between the songs there's some sporadic, meaningless chat. I concentrate on keeping his drink topped up for him. His monotonous voice becomes increasingly irritating as the night wears on.

What seems like hours later, he motions to Mi-Young, who is standing close by, so she comes over to our table to speak to him. Once their conversation has finished, she comes over to me and with steely eyes tells me to escort Mr Lee to the back room.

No, please don't do this to me again! Have some heart, woman. You cannot do this to me!

With both heart and soul fully against what is going to happen next, I pick up both glasses and the bottle of soju and escort him over to the dreaded burgundy curtains. As I draw ever closer to them my legs begin to feel heavy. I'm quaking in my heels. Barely able to stand without support, he stumbles along behind me.

Once we have gone through the curtains I see that one of the rooms is in use so I push open the vacant door which is slightly ajar. Fear grips me as I realise that it's the same room as the previous time.

Think positive!

I lead him into the room and we sit down on the couch. I pour some soju into both glasses and he raises a toast.

'To us.'

We clink glasses.

Guess I have to try this soju now.

'Who can drink fastest?' I ask, thinking on my feet.

'You want race?'

'Why not? Ready, steady, go!'

We both down it in one. The taste is as awful as I had imagined it would be, stinging the back of my throat as it works its way down towards my stomach.

'I never do this before,' he says. 'It fun. Again?'

133

I pour some more drink into both glasses, making sure that his is brimmed to the top and mine somewhat lower.

'This not fair. Look!' he protests as he notices the difference in levels just before we clink glasses.

'I'm just thinking about you,' I explain. 'I know it's your favourite and, as you know, I shouldn't be drinking during working hours. But I'm having fun with you so let's just drink, shall we?'

Hope that sounds convincing…

'Okay, just for you. You my special girl. Look so beautiful. One, two, three, go!' He gulps down the liquid and I knock mine back too, wincing at the dreadful taste. I'd like to spit it out but that's not an option so I chug it down.

He puts his glass down. 'Finish. I no want drink today but…' He laughs and slides his hand up my thigh to my knickers. 'I do anything for my girl.'

You keep on believing it, idiot!

I'm feeling distinctly light-headed as the alcohol begins to cast its spell.

Okay, no more soju. Keep him talking for as long as possible and the drink will take its effect.

I top up his glass again.

'No more soju for me,' I say as he goads me to drink some more. 'Now, tell me about your day at work.'

He starts telling me about some important business transaction but he's becoming incoherent and I have to ask him to repeat what he has said several times. This all eats up more precious time. Eventually, however, he looks at his watch and mumbles something in Korean then reaches out and starts fondling my breasts. Then he starts trying to take my dress off. I remove his hands and then stand up and unzip the dress so that it falls to the floor. I'm left wearing just some sexy red lingerie.

'Now your turn,' I tell him.

Yuck! Did I really just say that?

He gets up unsteadily and pulls off his jacket and tie. Then he unbuttons his shirt and, with some difficulty, removes his shoes. When he tries to take his trousers off he loses his balance while trying to stand on one leg and topples onto the massage couch. Clearly exasperated, he gets up again, with his trousers tangled around his ankles. Finally he lowers his pants and tries to arouse himself while looking at me.

Surely he can't get it up now given the state he's in?

He mumbles something in Korean, but cannot seem to get stimulated, no matter how much he's looking at my almost naked body. I sense that he's beginning to feel foolish standing there in front of me and he starts ranting away in Korean. I reassure myself that the walls are soundproof so nobody outside can hear what's going on.

Then he has an idea. He gets out his phone and gestures that I start playing with myself.

The sleaze bag!

Unable to think of any way out of it, I oblige and start putting my hand down my red panties and fumble away. He films everything in one hand, and in desperation tries to masturbate with the other, but nothing is happening down there for him. Unable to remain standing he plonks himself down on the sofa, still recording me. He abandons his attempts to get any life out of his shrivelled penis and starts to finger my clitoris. I feel violated as he prods at me without any preliminary caress even. My hands tremble as I wipe away a few tears that have escaped my eyes.

Get your fucking hand off me!

After five more disgusting minutes of him prodding me and pretending to be aroused he looks at his watch and gestures that he has to leave. I get dressed as quickly as I can, not wanting him to see me naked for a moment longer than absolutely necessary. He, however, is unable to put his own clothes back on properly so I help him out, not wanting this horrid experience to last a minute longer.

'See, you look smart now.' I congratulate him, but there's not much response from him as he reaches for the door handle.

I glance at the couch and see that his mobile phone is still lying there so as quick as a flash I swipe it, but then realise I have nowhere to put it. Fortunately it's a clamshell phone so I'm able to place it in the palm of my left hand and clench my fist over it so it's not readily visible. I put my other arm around his waist and guide him back into the club, making sure that my left arm stays behind my back.

Seeing that Mr Lee's in a terrible state again, Mi-Young rushes over to provide support and we sit him down at the bar. She then instructs me to go back to my table as she picks up the company phone and calls someone. Before I leave I blow Mr Lee a kiss and touch his cheek. This seems to surprise Mi-Young, who pauses and stares at me while in mid-conversation on the phone. Once back at the table I place the mobile between my crossed legs and am forced to sit it out.

Shortly afterwards, Mr Choi and Mi-Young walk Mr Lee out of the bar and I can afford to breathe a sigh of relief but it's short lived as Mi-Young darts her way over to my table.

'You don't fool me with kiss,' she whispers in my ear. 'You get him drunk! I no trust you.' She raises her hand as though she wants to slap me but with so many people still around she thinks better of it and strokes her hair instead. 'I watch you today, tomorrow and next day. I bring other customer to you.'

She is as good as her word, but all of the other clients that come to me that night just bore me to death.

'How long Korea?' says one.

Too bloody long.

'Do you like Korea men?' says another.

136

If only I could tell you…

I give diplomatic answers to fend them off and to keep my already bloodied nose clean. Then I remind myself of what the old man on the plane asked me. 'Do you like kimchi?' The memory makes me smile warmly for the first time in ages, reminding myself of happier times and the fact that there may after all be some decent men out there in this world…

The night finally ends and, feeling mightily tired, my attention returns to the mobile phone that has been safely tucked away between my legs all this time. While Mr Choi says his farewells to his colleagues and Mi-Young, I slip the mobile inside my knickers as it's the only place where I can hide it. Mr Choi comes over, gesturing that I should go upstairs now. As he escorts me to my cell I pray that the phone doesn't fall out or that he doesn't notice the phone's outline. Halfway upstairs I feel a strange sensation as the phone starts to vibrate. He stops walking and looks at me with a frown that makes me freeze. I feel my heart beating twice as fast.

'What that noise?' he asks gruffly.

'I can't hear anything. Maybe it's an insect or something.'

'No, I hear something,' he says, still frowning.

My heart leaps into my mouth as I do my best to remain poker-faced.

He starts patting his own pockets until he locates his own phone. He stares at it for some time, which only increases my anxiety.

'Ah, my new phone,' he says finally, seemingly satisfied that he's identified the source of the sound.

I look away and breathe a quiet sigh of relief, hoping fervently that Mr Lee's phone doesn't make any more noises.

We reach my room and Mr Choi opens the door and I go in. Then I turn around quickly.

'Wait! I need to go to the toilet,' I say with urgency.

'No time for this. Have to go,' he replies, looking decidedly unamused.

'You want me to pee in my pants?'

'Okay, okay. Be quick!' he snaps.

I go to the bathroom and close the door while he waits outside. Once in I quickly get the phone out of my knickers, pull them down to my ankles and sit on the toilet. I open up the phone but it is password protected.

Bugger!

I try to think of a plan B.

Where can I leave this? Think, God damn it, think!

Then I have an idea. I finish my business and flush the toilet. As the water cascades down into the bowl I bend down and peer behind the toilet. I jam the phone behind it, tight up against the pipe, where it cannot be seen, then wash my hands and leave the bathroom. He escorts me back to my room and locks me in.

I take off my clothes and look glumly at the bare bed without the duvet and pillows that I had before. I try to put that thought to one side and think about the phone, hoping that things might just be going my way for once.

If I can crack the password then I might just be able to get out of this terrible mess.

I get as comfortable as I can and close my eyes.

Chapter Twenty

'Wake up, wake up!'

This time it is Mr Yi who shakes me awake. Mr Choi, who's looking as menacing as usual, is standing behind Mr Yi, letting him do all the physical work.

'Get off me! Leave me alone,' I plead pathetically.

'Where is it?' Mr Choi demands.

'Where is what? I don't know what you're talking about,' I reply, suddenly feeling fully alert.

'You know what.'

He nods to Mr Yi, who duly obliges and shakes me again, more vigorously than before.

'Mr Lee lose phone last night,' Mr Choi continues. 'I think you take it.'

'No, I didn't take it. I don't know anything about it,' I lie.

Mr Choi comes closer, while Mr Yi, who has stopped shaking me, pins me down to the bed.

'I ask again. Where you put phone?'

'I don't know where it is! Search the room if you don't believe me,' I challenge him.

He considers what I've said and then says something to Mr Yi, who then grabs my arm and pulls me out of bed. My nightie gets caught and there's a ripping sound as he throws me to the floor. He then pulls the bed violently away from the wall and checks through the covers and all around the bed frame, even tearing out some of its wooden slats, but finally indicates to Mr Choi that there is nothing there.

Mr Choi says something else to Mr Yi so he searches the rest of the room. It doesn't take him long as there are very few places a mobile phone could be hidden. After rooting through the chest of drawers, unceremoniously throwing my clothes and my photo of Rachel and me onto the floor, he again shakes his head at Mr Choi.

'What you done with phone?' Mr Choi repeats angrily. He pulls his hand back and I fear that he's going to hit me.

'How many more times?' I whimper. 'You can't find it because I don't have it!'

His open hand connects hard with my right cheek. Unlike before, this time I hold my nerve and remain silent, which seems to aggravate him even more.

'If you lie me you in big trouble!' he yells, pointing towards Mr Yi.

He orders me to stay where I am while the two of them stand there discussing the situation. They are interrupted by a phone ringing. Mr Choi reaches into his pocket and answers it. A couple of minutes later he ends the call and places his phone back in his pocket. He says something to Mr Yi and they both leave the room, locking the door on their way out.

I'm left with a sore cheek, a bed that needs to be fixed and not knowing whether I'm going to be given any food today. In some pain, I slowly get up with the intention of trying to fix the bed at least. I pick up the photo of Rachel and me, which is lying on the floor. The glass is all smashed so I take the picture out of the frame and look at it intently, realising how important this single item is to me right now.

How I could do with your strength right now, Rach.

I place the picture back on the chest of drawers and try to fix the bed, without much success. Then I slump down on it and wait for the daily offering of cold rice and water. Nothing materialises. I double up on the mattress and try to ignore the hunger pangs. Terrible thoughts creep into my mind.

Perhaps I'm now surplus to requirements. All washed up like some old, past-her-sell-by-date prostitute. The others were right when they said I can't look after

myself. It was a terrible mistake to leave the UK.
Perhaps it would be best to end it all right here, right
now.

I scan the room for a potential means of killing myself but there's nothing obvious I can use. I examine the ceiling for any kind of hook that I can hang myself from but there's nothing up there either – and I wouldn't know how to do it properly anyway.

Out of sheer desperation I pick up a wooden slat and start smacking it against the floor, screaming at the top of my voice, but no matter how loud I scream nobody comes…

'What happen you?'

I open my eyes and rub them. Mr Choi is standing over me with a tray of food.

'You crazy girl. You cut hand.'

I look down and see dried blood on my hand.

He has a pack of tissues on him and starts cleaning my hand up, dipping a tissue in my cup of water to cleanse my wound. 'It okay. Don't worry. I fix everything.' He goes on to pick up the wooden slats and reinserts them in the bed.

'See? Just like new bed,' he says minutes later, helping me up from the mattress and placing it back on the bed. 'Eat food. I go and get something for hand,' he promises.

Why has he changed his tune so suddenly?

Desperate for food, I grab the tray and shovel handfuls of cold rice into my mouth, which tastes good for once. While I'm still eating, Mr Choi re-enters with some plasters and antiseptic wipes for my cut. He also has some make-up to disguise my sore cheek, where he slapped me earlier.

'Okay now? Use this.' He strokes my hair.

Get off me!

'Yes, I'm fine now.'

141

Like hell!

'Good. I need you look beautiful every day.' He kisses my damaged hand. 'No more this. I come back soon. Be ready.'

After he has gone I move towards the wall and scratch another line in it, then count how many days I've been here. Each time I hope the line I have scratched will somehow be my last, but I feel that my hopes of rescue are beginning to fade.

Chapter Twenty-one

While taking a shower, I think about the phone that's within touching distance right now but I'm agonisingly aware that without the password it isn't any good for anything. As the cold water cascades down my shivering body I can only wonder in frustration about Mr Lee's security details.

Later on that evening, Mr Choi has me cleaning glasses again at the bar while he holds yet another meeting at one of the tables with the hostess girls. I had a feeling that Mr Yi would be back on the scene today after he showed up in my bedroom earlier on and, sure enough, he's there to wield his authority on Mr Choi's behalf.

One of the girls, whom I don't recognise, stands up and seems to be introducing herself to the others.

She must be a replacement for Francesca.

Mr Choi says something that makes everyone laugh, but moments later the laughter stops and things seem to turn more serious as I see him show his mobile phone to everyone.

He must be asking them if anyone has seen Mr Lee's phone.

He works his way around the table, excluding the new girl, but judging by the sound of his voice he doesn't get the answer that he's looking for. His voice grows more irritable when he runs out of girls to question. The jovial atmosphere at the start of the meeting is a distant memory as he speaks severely to the whole group, evidently warning them to watch their step.

Once he's finished speaking, he gets up and heads off to his office with Mi-Young and Mr Yi in attendance. I see the blinds being pulled down in the office window.

It must be serious.

My attention is then drawn to the girls, who get up from the table and disperse themselves around the room, readying themselves for the opening of the club.

They aren't laughing tonight.

While the bartender disappears down to the storage room, presumably to get some more supplies, I put the glass that I'm cleaning on the bar and head off to the toilet. I open the door and head for the cubicle.

How long will they stay in the office? Is this an opportunity to escape maybe?

Then I recall something important.

Bugger! Mr Yi locked the door after all the girls arrived.

Hopeful becomes hopeless once again. I hear the main door to the ladies open and I jump up in panic, then flush the toilet and hope it's not Mi-Young, who's just walked in.

I open the cubicle door and see that it's the new arrival, who's preening her hair in the mirror. I stand next to her at the basin and wash my hands. She looks startled when I appear right next to her but then she shoots me a smile, revealing a perfect set of teeth, and says something in Korean.

'Sorry,' I tell her. 'I don't speak Korean.'

'You speak English?' she asks. 'Okay! I speak!'

'Oh, good,' I reply, smiling back at her.

'Me Seoyeon,' she says, offering her hand. 'I think you Russian.'

'Russian? Why?'

'Many Russian girls in Korea they do this work.'

'Oh, I see. I think we'd better get back to work,' I tell her. 'They don't like us to be in here too long.'

I dry my hands on the towel and then step towards the door but Seoyeon tugs at my arm so I turn around to face her.

'Wait, wait. Do I see your face somewhere?' she asks.

144

'I'm sorry but I've never seen you before in my life. You must have me muddled me up with someone else,' I tell her. 'We really have to get out of here.'

I make my way hurriedly back into the club, scanning the room for any sign of the big three, but the coast appears to be clear so I hasten to the bar and finish cleaning the final few glasses that are stacked up.

The office door opens a couple of minutes later and Mr Yi takes up his usual place at the main doors. Mi-Young comes out seconds later and arrows her way towards me. She chats to the bartender before turning her attention to me.

'If you have phone make no mistake. Big trouble!' she seethes.

'How many more times? I don't have the bloody phone!' I snap back.

'Remember who I am! Finish job and go to table.'

Looking slightly shaken at my dissent, she turns with a click of her heels and marches off to instruct the new girl.

The doors open and, as I'd predicted he would, Mr Lee appears among a number of other clients. Instead of allowing Mi-Young to show him to my table, however, he steps inside Mr Choi's office.

Hmm. I wonder what's going on in there?

A few minutes later Mr Lee re-emerges and is shown to my table. As usual, Mi-Young takes his jacket off him and goes to the bar to fetch his drink.

'Hi, Charlotte. How are you?'

Not the better for seeing you.

'Hello, Mr Lee. I'm good, thanks. How about you?'

'Very bad.' he says grumpily. 'I lose my phone last night. I look everywhere but cannot find.' He looks thoroughly depressed about the whole sorry situation, which gives me a secret inner glow of satisfaction.

'Oh dear, I'm sorry to hear that. The same thing happened to me once a few years ago. I was so upset, so

145

I know how you feel right now. Oh well, you can have a nice time with me tonight.'

Ha ha ha! Serves you right, you nasty little rapist!

He smiles for the first time and places his hand on my thigh. 'What happen?' he asks as he notices the plaster and slight bruising on my hand.

'Oh, I caught it in the door. Nothing to worry about.'

He nods his head, then changes the subject entirely. 'It my birthday today – but no kiss from wife yet.'

I'm not surprised!

'Well, happy birthday to my favourite client.' I kiss him on his cheek just as Mi-Young returns with the soju. She looks mystified by the intimacy she is witnessing.

'Thank you,' he says. 'Tonight I want nice time with you, but my childrens want see me so just short time together.' He looks a bit depressed again.

'Oh, I'm sure I can make your night a special one. Which song would you like me to sing?'

'My favourite. Beatles, of course.'

Don't you know anything else, you idiot?

I notice Seoyeon walk past as I go to the bar to collect the microphone. She's looking right at me but, remembering what happened to Francesca, I avoid eye contact with her. I get to the bar and collect the microphone from the bartender then return to Mr Lee and start singing.

After a few celebratory birthday drinks, he gets up and says that he's going home to see his children.

'My phone,' he says. 'It worry me. Many information. If you find, give back,' he requests.

'Yes, of course I will. You go and have a nice time with your wife and children.'

'Childrens yes, wife no. We no love each other any more.' He sounds disgruntled again. 'But I have you in my life and that make me happy. Very happy.'

Oh, for God's sake! Does he think he's in love with me or something?

146

'Try not to worry about your phone. I'm sure it will turn up soon.'

In the hands of the police if I have anything to do with it!

A quieter end to the night ensues with more than one hostess girl to each client, making me pretty much redundant as the majority of customers don't speak any English.

At long last the evening ends and Mr Choi takes me upstairs.

'You want toilet?' he asks as we arrive outside my cell.

'No, thanks.'

Best wait until tomorrow to use the phone. Don't want to arouse suspicion.

He shows me into my room and is just about to lock the door when he opens it again.

'Mr Lee talk about phone with you?'

'Yes, he did. He said he couldn't remember where he lost it. It could be anywhere.'

He nods slowly. 'Hmm. Now I tired so no time talk. We talk tomorrow.'

He closes the door and locks it. I get into bed, torn between relief and apprehension. Fortunately, the night is a little cooler than usual, which enables me to drift off to sleep more easily.

Chapter Twenty-two

The following morning Mr Choi lets me out of my room to take my daily shower. The thought of showering in icy, cold water always gives me a shudder but this morning I approach the ordeal with great anticipation.

I lock the bathroom door and get down on my hands and knees to see if Mr Lee's phone is still behind the toilet. I smile as I see that it's still there and take it out of its hiding place. I turn on the shower to cover the beeping sound the phone makes when it is opened up. Today's date flashes up on the screen and I see that there have been a number of missed calls from the same number, but then something more pressing draws my attention. The phone battery is running low. There's no time to waste! I hurriedly set about trying to crack the password.

My first few attempts are futile and I begin to worry that he's chosen a special date in Korea that I couldn't possibly guess. Then I remember that it was his birthday just yesterday and in growing desperation tap in the day and the month of the year. To my amazement I suddenly find I have gained access to the thing!

I try to remain calm and think of a number to call.

Come on, what's the country code for calls to the UK. Think!

I manage to remember it from a guidebook that Rachel gave me before I left, so tap in the code plus my parents' number and wait for a connection. The wait takes forever and I fear that in my haste I have tapped in the wrong number. I remove the phone from my ear and to my utter disbelief find myself looking at a blank screen. No battery!

Feeling absolutely crestfallen I collapse onto the floor and berate myself for not calling last night.

I don't know how much more I can take! Whatever did I do in my life to deserve this?

An impatient banging on the bathroom door quickly brings me back to my senses.

'What you doing? No time waiting all day. Hurry!'

I somehow get my act together and get the phone hidden behind the toilet once more before Mr Choi gets it into his head to break the door down. Then I flush the bowl and get in the shower.

'Sorry, I just needed the toilet,' I call through the door. 'I'll be out soon!'

I wrap my towel around me and open the door, upon which, to my horror, he rushes straight past me into the bathroom and closes the door. I wait in the corridor outside, my heart in my mouth.

What if he's looking for it?

In a state of utter confusion I stand there like a frozen statue and hold my breath. The seconds seem to pass by like hours as I await my fate.

What are you doing, woman? Here's your chance to escape, God damn it!

Then I hear the sound of the toilet flushing and the door opens.

Chance gone. You idiot!

He comes out, still doing up his flies. He looks at me intently, giving off angry vibes.

'Tonight we talk in office,' he informs me as he escorts me back to my cell and locks me in.

As the rest of the day slowly drags on, Mr Choi's parting words resonate in my head.

Why does he want to talk to me?

I stare at the lines I've scratched into the wall and add another one to the lengthening tally. It feels like I've been here for ever.

Why is no one looking for me? Has everyone forgotten about me?

149

I roll over in my bed and pick up the picture that Rachel gave to me.

What would you do, Rach? How would you get out of this mess that I'm in?

I place the photo face down on my chest as I try to dream up yet another escape plan.

What seems like hours later, I slowly rouse myself from the deep sleep I've slipped into. Then I realise Mr Yi is there, prodding me awake.

'Wake up! Work start soon. Wear this.'

He chucks a bag onto the bed and retreats to the bedroom door, from where he watches my every move with hawk-like eyes. I take off my clothes and slip on my dress I find in the bag.

'Come, come. Boss waiting downstairs,' he barks at me.

He frogmarches me out of the room and down to the club. Mr Choi is sitting on a chair at the bar, evidently waiting for me.

'Charlotte, look at you!' he exclaims as I approach. He grabs me and kisses me on my cheek.

I try to hold my breath but the stench of stale cigarettes is far too powerful and wafts up my nose, making me cough.

'You sick?' he asks with some concern.

I shake my head.

Smelly git!

'Good! Sickness mean no money for me. We go office now,' he says cheerily.

He says something to Mr Yi, who nods his head and goes to the main doors, and then escorts me towards his office. He reaches out to tap in the code for the door but fails to cover his hand properly and, hardly believing my luck, I get an unobstructed view of what he's doing.

Two, zero, zero, eight!

He opens the door and gestures at me to step in.

'Sit down,' he instructs me, suddenly businesslike. He goes to the window and pulls down the blind, then walks back to his desk and places a mobile phone on the table. Trying to remain composed, I check it to see if it's Mr Lee's or not.

'So why am I here?' I ask, my voice wavering and my hands trembling.

He clenches his fist. 'What you done?'

I look at him confused.

'You not know?' He lifts his clenched fist up and bangs it on the table repeatedly. Then he gets up from his chair and moves closer to me. My thoughts quickly turn to the phone and where I hid it and whether it was the safest of places or not.

'Mi-Young say that you no respect last night! She say you anger her.'

Phew. Is that all?

'Do you know why?' I counter. 'I can tell you.'

He nods.

'She thinks I took Mr Lee's phone but I honestly don't know what happened to it. You have to believe me!'

He growls and looks me directly in the eyes. 'One last time. Did you take he phone? Yes or no?'

Spittle shoots out of his mouth and lands on my face. I wipe it off very deliberately.

'No, I did not,' I tell him firmly, emphasising each word.

He stares at me for a few seconds longer as though checking whether I'm telling the truth or not. I hold my expression of indignant innocence. The pressure is so intense that I feel like my head is going to explode.

Finally he looks away and I sink back into the chair. He walks back to his side of the desk, sits down and toys with the phone in front of him for a few moments. I sense that he's weighing up his options.

'Okay. Apologise Mi-Young later. Go now and welcome Mr Lee when come here.'

151

I leave the office and as there is nobody other than Mr Yi around, head straight for the toilet. Once inside I stand in front of the sink and wash my face, scrubbing hard at my skin to get every last trace of my captor's saliva off it. I hear the door open just as I'm drying myself with a towel. I half expect Mi-Young to be standing behind me, but then I see it is Seoyeon.

'Charlotte Dunn?' she says.

I freeze, everything in my head going deathly still. She knows my name. I don't know what to do next.

'No, that's not me,' I murmur.

I look away but she steps in front of me to see my face at close quarters.

'It is you, isn't it? My God! I recognise you before! I check last night on BBC website.'

What? I'm on the BBC website?

'No, no,' I splutter. 'I'm sorry, you're wrong. Like I told you yesterday – you must have mistaken me for someone else.'

'Listen. I'm not like bimbos out there. I am uni student. I see your face on news. I know it.' Seoyeon isn't to be so easily shaken off, I discover.

I shut my eyes for a moment, trying to work out how best to put her off. She could get us both killed. 'Now, you listen to me. Don't get involved. It's none of your business! Just stay out of it!' It occurs to me that the others probably don't realise she speaks English and might talk to me – if they should find out... 'Do *they* know you can speak English?'

'No. I choose that way. My parents very angry if know I do this job but I need money to pay for education. I no stupid. I want help you. Please let me help,' she begs.

'No!' I hiss. 'Look, it's too dangerous! Please don't speak to me ever again. Just stay out of my way. End of! I'm doing this for your own good, believe me,' I warn her.

152

I step quickly towards the door and open it to see the other girls just arriving, chatting away and laughing. I go over to the bar, where Mi-Young is talking to the bartender, and wait patiently until he goes down to the storage room, then seize the moment.

'Mi-Young?'

She turns her head. 'Yes?'

Here goes. Nip it in the bud.

'I'm sorry for how I spoke to you last night. I was wrong and hope you can forgive me.'

She looks at me for some time before saying anything, relishing my anguish for as long as possible.

'I your boss. In Korea respect for older person important, yes?'

I nod meekly under her laser-beam stare. 'I'm really sorry. What can I do to help you tonight before we open?'

She pauses, then seems to accept the apology. 'I have perfect job for you. Help barman bring drinks up. I show you now.'

I smile gratefully. 'Yes, I'll do it. I promise it won't happen again.'

What a bitch!

She leads me down the storage room stairs. She says something in Korean to the bartender, who hands me a crate of soju to carry upstairs. I kick off my high heels, leaving them next to the bottom stair, and follow the empty-handed Mi-Young back up while quietly cursing her name as the weight takes its toll on my arms. Once back in the bar she beckons me to put the crate down on the floor and go back down to bring another one up.

'New job for you every night,' she promises me. Then she turns to one of the hostess girls and says something to her, clearly about me. They both laugh at my predicament.

Bitches, the lot of ya!

While I'm carrying the second crate upstairs I'm taken back to my job at the supermarket, when I used to put tins of cat food out on the shelves. I'd hated all that so much then. Life at the supermarket seems like paradise to me now, unlike this one that I am currently trapped in. I remember the conversation I had with Liz and the advice she gave me – *Give them a call! I know I would.* A single teardrop runs down my cheek as I remember how excited I'd been making that call to Mr Bliss. And it had all led to this hellhole. I dump the crate down next to the other one.

'Careful! Okay. Go to table now,' snaps Mi-Young as the first clients come through the main doors.

She tells me to hurry up so I retrieve my high heels and retreat to my usual spot to await the first client of the evening.

As the night goes on the bar fills up to almost bursting point. As a consequence Mi-Young is sending clients my way, who seem to be generally disinterested and unable to utter even a word of English, just because there aren't enough girls to go around. Eventually Mr Lee makes an appearance, and Mi-Young politely requests the man I'm currently trying but failing to entertain to move on to pastures new. The man, who seems to be utterly transfixed by her, nods and complies, following her like a well-trained puppy to another table.

'Mr Lee, how great to see you! I've been waiting for you. Please sit down.'

Mi-Young, who has now returned, eyes me suspiciously as she collects his jacket and glides off to the bar.

'So happy see you,' he responds.

'So how was your birthday? Nice to see the children?'

'Oh, yes. They buy me nice presents.'

'Oh, good. How about your wife?'

His smile falters. 'Don't talk about her.'

'I'm sorry. I won't mention her again.'

154

Pity the poor woman.

He puts his hand on mine. 'I want nice time with you tonight. I go out earlier after work.'

I catch the office door opening and Mr Choi emerges, on his way out through the main doors.

'You seem no here,' he remarks.

'Sorry. Something distracted me for a moment.' I gaze into his eyes. 'I'm all yours now. So, where did you go?'

'Just restaurant, with business partner.'

Mi-Young comes over with the drinks and bows to Mr Lee before she leaves. I pour him a large glass of soju, making sure it is filled to just below the brim. He takes a large swig.

Good boy, knock it back!

Then I get an idea, a likely way to get him to drink himself incapable once more.

'Did you enjoy the drinking game the other night?'

'Drinking game other night? I forget,' he says, looking baffled.

So I remind him of the game we played.

'Oh yes, drinking game. Yes, why not? But means you drink too. Maybe our secret,' he adds, knowing full well that I shouldn't get drunk while on the job.

'Well, Mr Lee, you have your drink and I'll go and get mine from the bar.'

'Oh, I think you call me Min-Jun now.' His smile broadens, which makes me feel sick to the pit of my stomach.

I get up and walk to the bar, which is packed with clients drinking and smoking before they are seated with a glamour girl. The bartender is busy serving clients right down at the other end. While I wait I feel my dress being tugged around the waist. I turn around and see Seoyeon next to me. I look around to see if anyone is watching us.

'Stay out of it!' I hiss.

155

'Your parents – they worried about you. How can I do nothing?'

She's pulling effectively at my heart strings but she doesn't appreciate the risk she is taking.

'Look, you don't know what they're capable of here!' I whisper. 'I'm not going to tell you again. Keep out of it!'

She looks confused, but I move away from her, just as the bartender spots me waiting. He mimes a microphone but I shake my head. Instead I point to a bottle of water in one of the fridges behind him. He gets it and pours some in a glass for me. I avoid eye contact with Seoyeon as I brush my way past her, concentrating upon not spilling anything from the glass.

I arrive back at my table to find Mr Lee is playing with his phone.

Oh, shit, he's found the phone!

'Did you find your phone?' I say, trying to hide my anxiety as I sit down.

'This new phone,' he explains. 'Look like old one, but much better.'

Relief washes over me. 'Oh, that's good. At least you have one.'

'Yes, but lose many information.' He suddenly looks downcast.

'Don't lose hope. Cheer up, you never know, it might turn up one day.'

He sighs. 'I want forget. Now I here with you. Teach me drinking game.'

I talk him through it as the noise in the club steadily increases. The place is becoming quite boisterous. A lot of the noise is coming from a group of businessmen at the bar, who are downing shots of alcohol and puffing away on cigarettes.

'How about truth or dare?' I suggest to him. 'That's even more fun.'

He hesitates for some time before asking me to explain the rules. I spend a couple of minutes explaining and when he's got it I ask him to choose which he'd like. He tells me he wants a dare, so I dare him to drink two fingers' worth of soju, which he does with ease. Next it's my turn. I opt for truth.

'Do you have boyfriend in UK?'

I'm taken aback by his question and find myself thinking about Joe.

'Just one.'

He looks at me intently and I can see he's instantly jealous. 'You still love him?'

'Oh, no. I did once but not now,' I say confidently.

'So no contact now?'

'We've finished. I don't want to see him ever again. I hate him and I–' I break off.

Pull yourself together, woman, before you blow it!

'And what? Tell me.'

I shrug. 'What does it matter? I'm here now with you.' I give him a fake smile and he places his hand on mine and gives it a gentle squeeze.

'Okay, so it's your turn again,' I remind him. The group of men at the bar are getting even rowdier, downing yet more shots of alcohol.

He develops a nervous twitch, reinforcing my prediction that he'll be reluctant to divulge any information about his personal life. Sure enough, he plumps for another dare so this time I tell him to drink four fingers. He baulks at first but eventually gives in and knocks it back, then belches loudly.

'Four too much,' he complains.

'Well, why don't you tell me something about yourself instead?'

The twitch reappears, making his right eye close.

The noise is making it really difficult to have a conversation. I glance towards the bar to see what's happening. Two men appear to have challenged each

157

other to see how many shots they can down. The others standing around them are egging them on, slapping them on their backs.

'See, Min-Jun? You should be more like them. They're enjoying life.'

He watches them for a moment and then refocuses on me. 'They are stupid. Low-level worker. Now you turn,' he says grumpily.

I opt for a dare this time. He laps it up, requesting I down half of my drink, which I do straightaway.

'Wow, amazing!' he breathes.

'Are you impressed with my drinking skills?'

For an answer he leans over and kisses me on my cheek. I pull back and cough into my hands as the smell of cigarette smoke fills my nostrils.

'You sick?' he asks with concern.

'No, I'm fine. Come on then, your turn. Truth or dare?'

He goggles at me as the soju begins to take effect. His twitch returns and he doesn't take up the challenge to tell the truth so I top up his glass with soju and dare him to drink half of it.

'Aww, Charlotte, you devil!' He moves his hand towards my waist and tries to tickle me but I move farther away from him.

'Later, Min-Jun,' I say, winking at him.

I knock back some more of my drink and he lets out a laugh.

'If you can then of course I can. I not lose to woman!'

He raises the glass and drinks half of its contents. After putting it down his facial expression tells me all is not well. He excuses himself and heads off to the toilet, but on his way bumps heavily into one of the clients, who has been busily downing drinks with his mates at the bar. Pushing and shoving between the two ensues as the argument gets heated. Wayward punches are thrown as the two drunken men start hitting out into thin air. The hostess girls and clients nearby stop their chatter and watch to see what will happen next. Mr Lee finally lands one on the chin of the other client and is then restrained by the man's mates, who pin his arms behind his back while he struggles to break free.

Mr Yi suddenly appears and tries to take control of the situation by pointing at the main door, seemingly ordering the group of friends to leave the premises. One of them, however, lashes out and lands a punch on Mr Yi's cheek. The noise in the bar rises another notch. Mr Yi shouts something at the top of his voice and the place falls silent.

The balance of control now firmly in his favour, Mr Yi waves the knot of drunks over to the main door and drives them all out into the street. The bar is now almost empty, so the hostess girls rush to the main door like a herd of bambis to see what's going on outside. I join them and see that the fighting is continuing unabated, with Mr Yi in the thick of things, trying to protect Mr Lee from the rest, who are now baying for blood.

Should I take my chance?

While everyone is distracted by the commotion, I sneak to the office and see through the window that it's vacant. Within seconds I am tapping the secret code into the lock. I cross my fingers, and to my amazement I hear the mechanism work.

Yes!

One final look at the others reveals that I've been spotted by Seoyeon, but she just smiles before turning back to the entertainment outside. I hesitate for a moment, realising I am relying utterly on Seoyeon's discretion, but the adrenaline that is rushing through me persuades me to turn the knob and without anyone else noticing I slip surreptitiously into the office, closing the door behind me.

I hurriedly make my way towards Mr Choi's desk and pick up the phone. Remembering the country code for the UK from the other day, I tap in the number and wait.

'Hello?'

She's in!

'Mum, it's me,' I whisper.

There's a gasp at the other end. 'Charlotte! Oh, my God! You're alive!' She sounds stunned with surprise.

The familiarity of her voice threatens to overwhelm me with emotion, but I know this isn't the time to give in to it.

'Ssh, Mum! Listen! I'm in trouble and I don't have much time.'

'You're in trouble. I knew it!'

'Just listen, would you? I've been kidnapped.'

'Kidnapped?' Horror replaces condemnation in her voice.

'When I end this call,' I press on, 'inform the police straightaway.'

'Oh, God, Charlotte!' she cries. 'What's happened to my little girl?'

'Mum, concentrate! I don't have much time. Wait a sec...'

I put the phone down and peek through the office window. The girls are still looking outside but then I see Mi-Young brushing her way back in past the mob at the entrance. I quickly return to the desk and pick up the phone.

'Mum, I have to go. I love you both.'

Mum is still blubbing uncontrollably as I place the phone down on the handset.

I hear the key code being tapped in so I duck down and hide under the desk. The tell-tale clicking of heels tells me that it must be Mi-Young, who has entered the room. She moves towards the desk and picks up the phone while getting comfortable in the chair, crossing her legs and rotating one foot in the air, narrowly missing my right arm.

She appears to be in some distress as she speaks loudly to the recipient, whom I presume to be Mr Choi. I hear her say Mr Lee's name and then mine, which sends a chill down my spine as I try to fathom out what she's saying. I think about the amount of alcohol Mr Lee has consumed and wonder whether she's telling my captor that I plied him with soju and deserve all the blame.

I feel a tickle in my throat and try to resist the urge to cough. To add to my alarm she drops a pen, which lands on the floor near my face. She stops speaking and her hand suddenly appears, feeling her way around for it. I quickly push the pen closer to her hand and wait, praying that she doesn't get down on her hands and knees to find it. Moments later she touches it with her pinkie and picks it up. I breathe a silent sigh of relief as she continues speaking on the phone. Finally she puts the phone down, then gets up and heads for the door.

Once the door is closed I'm forced to make a quick decision. I get up and try the other door behind the desk but there's another keypad so I move to the window, peeking around the edge to see what's happening in the club. It's still empty inside and I can just about see her making her way back to the entrance.

Just a bit longer.

She goes outside so I take my chance, hoping that the girls will still be goggled-eyed at the sight of a bunch of testosterone-fuelled men smacking nine bells out of each other. I open the door and nip quietly out, shutting it behind me. Having moved away from the office, I glance once more towards the main doors and see the others still transfixed by events outside, so I decide to go to the bathroom for a well-earned breather.

I open the door and walk towards the wash basin. A toilet flushes then a cubicle door opens and Seoyeon joins me at the basins.

'I saw you,' she says.

'You saw nothing, okay?' I reply sharply.

'Who were you talking to?'

'I'm sorry. What are you talking about?'

'I walked past the office on my way to toilet and see you on phone.'

'None of your business! Like I said before, stay away from me.' I can feel my temper slowly rising as I realise she knows all too much about me – and the danger that this could be putting both of us in.

'I make it my business. I don't like what's happening here. It's not right and I want to help you.'

I stare at her. There is no mistaking the concern she feels for me. I begin to feel myself relenting to her.

'Okay. But this is the last time we talk. I don't want anything bad to happen to you, so can you promise me?'

'I promise.'

'In case something bad happens to me, I want you to know this. There's a lake about an hour away from here. There are two bodies in that lake and *he* put them there.'

'Oh, my God! Who's *he*?'

'Mr Choi!'

Seoyeon looks shocked, as though she's beginning to realise the full extent of what she has got herself into.

'You see now why I didn't want to involve you in this?' I ask her.

She nods her head and looks subdued, then she sparks back into life.

'You know, there are many lakes around Seoul. What else can you tell me about it?'

I rack my brains. 'It was dark. Really dark. The roads were terribly bumpy and really narrow. I remember the road number was 78 and we were near a place called Sinsan-Ri. He said the lake was one of the deepest in Korea and there was a lit-up building next to it. Oh, and something about the lake being unlucky so people don't go there. He also owns a house about thirty minutes away from the lake. That's all I know.'

'Okay. I check on the net to see where you mean. Anything else?'

'Oh, yes. Mr Lee's old phone's hidden upstairs – but I don't have time to explain right now.'

'I'm sorry, who is Mr Lee?'

'He's a client who comes here.' I begin to worry about the length of time we've been gone for. 'Please leave here now and we must never speak again. Remember, don't say a word to anyone who works here.'

'Surely you tell by now that I'm not stupid. I promise I won't say anything and I try to help as much as I can. Good luck.' She moves closer and hugs me briefly. Then she walks out of the bathroom, leaving me feeling that I finally have a faint glimmer of hope.

I give it a minute or two before following her out. I look across to the entrance, where the girls are still peering out of the window so I go across to join them but soon realise I've missed the main action as the men are beginning to disperse. Mr Yi comes back in and beckons all of the girls except me over to him. Mi-Young, meanwhile, escorts me to the office. She taps in the code and gestures me to walk in, closing the door behind her. She then pulls the blinds down over the window and looks at me in disdain for a moment before grabbing me by the back of my head and thrusting her face into mine.

'Mr Lee very drunk. I think you responsible. We close early because you! Why you do this?'

'He was drunk before he even set foot in this place!' I retort, trying to deflect the blame.

As quick as a flash she draws her hand back and slaps me across the face. I yelp as the stinging sensation spreads across my left cheek. She grabs me by the back of my head again and plays with my hair.

163

'You think you smart girl. Such a pretty face with blonde hair and blue eyes – but no brain!' She slaps me around the face with such force that it knocks me to the floor. 'Get up, stupid girl!' she commands as she prods me with her shiny red shoe. 'Mr Choi come soon. He want speak to you. So you clean bar now before he come.'

I remain on the floor so she prods me again with more force, ordering me back to my feet. I stand up again with some difficulty. She opens the door. 'Go now!'

Still feeling groggy, I stumble out of the office and set about collecting the dirty glasses from the tables while she approaches Mr Yi, who is still talking to the rest of the girls.

I have just finished putting all the dirty glasses on the bar when Mr Choi enters the club via the main entrance. He walks past me with a face of thunder and starts talking with Mr Yi and Mi-Young. He then addresses the other girls, who shortly afterwards get up, bow their heads to him, and follow each other like sheep to the cloakroom to get their belongings. As Seoyeon passes me, she flashes me a warm smile that brings me some comfort in the face of the rollicking I expect imminently from our fearsome boss.

Mr Choi marches over to the bartender and mutters something to him. The bartender promptly abandons his post and gets his coat. The big three then form a close huddle, discussing things noisily for a few minutes while I hang about waiting at the bar. I hear my name mentioned several times, which does nothing to lessen the tension I feel – but I hold on to the thought that some positive things have happened this evening and that helps me keep a grip on myself.

Once the talking has finished, Mi-Young goes to the office and comes out with her coat on. She bows her head to her employer and with her poise still intact, glides out of the club. The two men then turn their attention to me, stalking over to where I'm standing.

'Mi-Young say you cause more trouble for me,' Mr Choi snaps. 'I no tolerate it any more! Come with me.'

Mr Yi grabs me and forces me to follow Mr Choi into the office. My struggles are pitiful in the face of his strength. He pushes me down onto a chair and stands behind me with his hands placed on my shoulders. Mr Choi, who has the phone in his hand, is tapping in some numbers on the handset. His glacial stare and the weight of Mr Yi's hands make me feel uneasy. Finally Mr Choi gets through to whoever he's calling and there's a brief conversation. Then he places the handset down and takes a moment to consider.

'Very interesting conversation with Mr Lee,' he tells me eventually. He seems to be revelling in my state of ignorance of the outcome of their conversation. The gold lumps appear one by one. 'You very lucky girl. He say he still want you so you still useful to me.' He moves over to my side. 'I tired of you and your games. This last chance. No more! This place now, many people here but look, nobody here because of you!' He is shouting now and his hand turns into a fist. He punches his desk without flinching. 'Last chance! Understand?'

I nod my head. He says something to Mr Yi, who grabs me and takes me upstairs to lock me in my cell for yet another long night.

As I lie there on the bed, I clutch my picture of Rachel and me close to my chest and think about the future and what it might bring before eventually drifting off to sleep.

Chapter Twenty-three

'Jeans and tee-shirt and still look beautiful,' Mr Choi observes as he sips his cup of coffee at the bar.

'Why have I been brought here so early this evening?' I ask him nervously.

He guides me behind the bar and tells me to follow him down the stairs to the storage room. At the bottom of the stairs he turns around and looks at me.

'You cause me much problem so I think what I do to get you stop playing game. Can't sleep last night. Too busy think you and why you no listen me. So I think much idea.'

He points towards the other end of the storage room, where there are a load of mixed-up boxes and crates that have been stacked up to about the same height as me. I can see a pair of large double doors and my mind begins to wander about what is on the other side. Then he walks me over to another area of the room that is better organised, with a much smaller stack in which the boxes and crates are neatly arranged by brand.

'Mi-Young say you very good last night. Bring bottles to the bar, she say. I want you move box from there to here.'

I feel my already depleted energy levels sink lower still as I realise what he has in store for me.

He strokes my cheek. 'Finish one hour!' He gives my cheek a vicious squeeze and with that he lets go of me and goes back upstairs.

I rub my cheek, which is still sore from the previous night, and go towards the newly delivered consignment, wondering how on earth I'm going to be able to cope with the task in hand. I walk up to the metal double doors, dreaming of an unlikely escape, but my hopes are dashed when I see a padlocked chain placed around the door handles. Feeling down and not wanting to displease him any further, however, I set about removing the cellophane wrapping from the new delivery.

About a third of the way through the job, I sit down to take a breather when I hear the door being opened upstairs. I hear footsteps coming down so I quickly jump up and pick up the box that I was sitting on. Having made his way down the stairs, the bartender spots me struggling with the heavy box but does nothing to offer me any assistance. He stares at me blankly for a second or two before picking up some things that he was looking for and makes his way back upstairs. After the door is closed again I put the box down in its correct place and sit back down on it, my aching bones telling me that I can do no more.

The hour almost up, I hear Mr Choi calling my name as he descends the stairs. I meet him at the bottom.

'You finish job?' he asks.

'I'm sorry, I really tried but I couldn't finish it,' I tell him apologetically.

He looks across at the stack that I should have shifted by now. A good third of it is still unpacked.

'What this?' he demands, with a growl. 'No good, no good.'

I see his hand begin to form into a fist.

'Do you want me to be tired when Mr Lee arrives?' I point out, trying my best to appease him.

He considers what I have said. I can almost hear him counting his notes.

'Okay. Mr Yi take you upstairs to room. Shower and wear nice dress.' He examines my sore cheek with his hand. 'Mi-Young strong woman!' he laughs. 'Wear make-up too. You finish job tomorrow.'

You're a nasty piece of work. I hate you!

Once back in the bar, Mr Choi beckons over Mr Yi, who then escorts me upstairs to get ready for the night.

167

I'm sitting all alone at my usual table when out of the corner of my eye I spot Mi-Young walking towards me with a client, who doesn't look familiar.

More mindless chat coming my way, no doubt.

He's a slimly built middle-aged man dressed in a natty dark suit. Mi-Young pulls out a chair and gestures for him to take a seat. Then she takes his coat and bows to him before walking off towards the cloakroom.

'Hello, I haven't seen you in here before. Is this your first time?' I ask him.

'Hi. Yes, it's my first time. I'm new to the area,' he replies, poker-faced.

Mi-Young comes back to our table with his drink. She asks him a question while smoothing out her red sequined dress, which clings to her curvaceous body. He answers and she leaves us alone.

I pour my client a drink.

'So you're new to the area, aren't you?'

'Yes, I recently moved to an apartment close by.' He picks up his glass and sips his drink, the level barely going down, then replaces it on the table.

'So you might be coming here a lot then?'

'Yes, I could be. What is your name?'

'I'm Charlotte.'

He raises his eyebrows. 'It's a pretty name. Where are you from?'

'Can't you tell?'

'I have an idea.'

'And what is your idea?'

'The UK, perhaps?'

'Got it in one.'

I look at him closely but he remains without expression, keeping his cards close to his chest.

'Your English is very good. Where did you learn it?'

'I studied abroad for a while. My teacher taught me the importance of learning languages. I'm eternally grateful to him. Can you speak Korean?'

I wish!

'Sadly not. I regret it a lot.'

He gives me a penetrating stare. 'Why do you regret it?'

'Well, you know. It's useful, right? Buying things at supermarkets, ordering food. That sort of thing.'

'Yes', he agrees. 'So how do you cope if you cannot speak Korean?'

I look up and catch Mr Lee walking into Mr Choi's office. My mind starts to wander.

'Charlotte? Are you okay?'

'Oh – yes, yes. Sorry. What did you say again?'

'I said, how do you cope?'

'I have friends who help me. They're really great.'

All of a sudden he takes his mobile phone from his pocket, apologises to me and answers it. I sit there waiting patiently for him to end the call, which he does soon afterwards.

'Sorry, it was an important call,' he tells me.

I'm vaguely intrigued to know what the call was about, but daren't risk saying something out of place and getting into yet more trouble with the boss. Then I spot Mi-Young coming towards us, so say nothing further to him. She chats to my client for some time before drawing his attention to another table, where two of the other girls are sitting without any clients. They in turn give my client a wave. He says something in reply to Mi-Young and gestures towards me several times. I'm perplexed as to what they are talking about. Eventually, however, I work out that Mi-Young is insisting on him joining the two girls at the other table. I don't know how she is putting it, but he clearly feels he has no choice and at last he agrees. He looks extremely disappointed as he bids me farewell and is shown to the other table. The two girls are all over him at once.

Mi-Young heads back to me. 'Mr Choi say he want speak with you in office. Follow me.'

I follow her over to the office. A large group of rowdy, drunken clients are just entering the bar. At the door, she covers the keypad and taps in the secret code. The door opens and she waves me in but remains outside herself, closing the door firmly after I've gone in.

Mr Choi is sitting at his desk. Mr Lee is seated in a chair opposite him.

'Charlotte. How are you?'

Mr Lee gets up from his chair and steps towards me. His eye is still badly bruised from last night's fight. He hugs me and, as I'm in Mr Choi's presence, I feel obliged to play along.

'Ouch! Your eye looks terrible. I'm really sorry about what happened last night.'

Should have been punched harder!

He laughs it off. 'It okay, no problem.'

Mr Choi pulls up another chair and invites me to sit down next to him. I notice a large brown envelope lying next to Mr Lee's hand.

'We talk about you this night,' says a smiling Mr Choi with his eyes firmly fixed on mine. 'We think good that you–'

He breaks off as we are all distracted by a burst of noise from the bar. He gets up quickly from his chair to look through the window. I catch a glimpse of a couple of police officers in full riot gear rushing in at the far end of the bar. He pulls the blind down rapidly and then rushes to his desk, opens the drawer and produces a pair of gloves, which he hastily pulls over his hands. Then, while we are still gaping at him, he takes out a gun. His smile long gone, he turns to the door that's directly behind his desk and punches in a code. The door opens and he gestures urgently with the gun for both of us to follow him. As we get up we hear the other door being rattled furiously from the other side. He orders us in no uncertain terms to hurry up.

'Don't worry!' Mr Lee tells me. 'I will not let anything bad happen to you!'

He grabs my hand and I can feel it shaking badly. I try to wriggle free but then I notice Mr Choi pointing his gun at me and decide this is no time to resist. Mr Choi points at the envelope on the desk with his free hand and says something in Korean to Mr Lee, who picks the envelope up and stashes it in his pocket.

As we rush out of the office I hear someone speaking through what sounds like a megaphone but Mr Choi chooses to ignore whatever's being said and slams the door shut behind us. We run along a dark, narrow corridor until we come to another door and then find ourselves at the top of a metal stairwell. I realise we are looking down into the near empty underground car park. Memories of the night Francesca's body was dumped in the lake come flooding back to haunt me.

Mr Choi urges both of us into the back of his car, then starts up the engine and puts his foot down, the tyres screeching on the concrete as he weaves his way through the car park and towards the ramp to the street outside. Mr Lee grips my hand to comfort me, but his own is sweaty and still shaking, so I don't feel comforted at all.

We reach the end of the ramp and Mr Choi brings the car to a halt before the automatic door so he can wind down his window and stick his gloved hand out to press the button. There is a moment of calmness for us all to collect our thoughts as the door slowly rises. Mr Lee lets go of my hand and wipes his brow with a handkerchief. I hold my breath, half hoping that there will be a cordon of police on the other side of the door.

But my luck is out once again. There are no police present and once the door is fully open he drives out into the street, turning right. He keeps to a respectful speed so as to avoid drawing unwanted attention. I stare out of the window for any signs of rescue, but all I can see is a quiet side street, with just a few cars parked along it. I notice a car's headlights go on just before I turn my head back, which raises my hopes that the authorities might be onto us after all, but then I realise it could be anyone in the car. I feel a sweaty hand being placed on mine once more but in my disappointment I cannot bring myself to look at Mr Lee's unattractive, perspiring face.

Mr Choi laughs. 'Police in this country no good!'

He clearly thinks he's got away with it. Perhaps he wants to rub it in that there's no chance of me being saved, even as I look out of the window in the hope of seeing flashing lights and hearing sirens closing in on us.

As we head into a busier district, I begin to wonder if we're following the same route that Francesca and I took the night we tried to escape. There are people everywhere enjoying the nightlife. For a moment I'm mesmerised by the neon lights on the sides of the buildings but then I feel Mr Lee's breath on my skin and am forced to remember the perilous situation that I find myself in.

'Soon we together,' Mr Lee murmurs as he puts his hand in his pocket and pulls out the brown envelope. 'I buy you so can be together. We live together,' he tells me joyfully.

I stare at him in horror and confusion. 'Are you crazy?' I burst out. 'You're married! This'll never work!'

'I no care them. Want you. I buy place for live. Just me and you.'

'And what about your children? Have you forgotten about them?'

His face changes, making me think that I've touched a raw nerve. 'My childrens mean everything to me. No say them.' He puts the envelope back in his pocket and places his hand on my thigh. 'You more to me.'

Now I feel totally spooked. I can't keep my emotions under lock and chain a moment longer. 'And what about me in all of this? *Your* plan. Listen to yourself – you,

172

you, *you*!' I'm shouting at him now as my anger and my outrage take over. 'What about *me*? What about *my* family? You only care about *you*!'

Mr Lee recoils in shock, as though he has never been answered back to in his life by a woman before. He takes his hand off my thigh and cowers in his seat, closing his eyes.

Mr Choi glares at me in the rear view mirror. He turns around and is in the process of ordering me to be quiet when a siren goes off suddenly nearby. We all stare ahead of us, one in hope, two in despair, as a large vehicle bears down on our car. But it only carries on past us, not even slowing.

'Only ambulance!' Mr Choi cries out. 'What I say you? Police no good!' He bellows with laughter.

I slump into the back seat, overcome with despair.

Chapter Twenty-four

Eventually we turn onto a busy highway that runs through the city. I fear that the chance for me to be found by the police has all but gone. Once out of the city, we pass a large road sign and, as I have anticipated, I see we are heading towards Sinsan-Ri.

Mr Lee is resting his head on the headrest and looks utterly exhausted from the night's exertions. Mr Choi, in contrast, is humming to himself as we cruise along the road, seemingly without a care in the world.

Eventually we come to a standstill. The headlights shine on a pair of large gates, which I vaguely recognise. Mr Choi presses a button inside his car and they open slowly. Revving up the engine again, we drive through them and go down a steep slope.

I think I know where I am now.

We reach a door which opens automatically and drive into a large garage.

'You know this place, Charlotte?' Mr Choi gives a low laugh, which stirs Mr Lee from his exhausted slumber.

Flashbacks of Francesca's battered face linger in my mind as Mr Choi parks the car and turns the engine off. The two men get out. Mr Choi opens the door for me and shouts at me to follow him. He closes the door once I'm out, then turns me around and handcuffs me before marching me down the same narrow corridor I remember from last time. Finally he opens the door we arrive at and pushes me into the room beyond. It is the room where Francesca died.

The two men follow me in. Mr Choi makes me sit down on one of the two chairs and then sets about tying me to it while Mr Lee lingers a few feet away. Once he's satisfied that I'm secure he speaks.

'Why police come to club?' he demands. I can tell that despite his apparently relaxed demeanour in the car, he is absolutely seething.

I remain tight lipped.

'Why police come?' he repeats, slapping my face hard.

I yelp at the pain of the blow. Mr Lee starts to say something but Mr Choi rounds on him, yelling and waving his gun in the air.

'Last chance!' he shouts, turning on me again. 'Why police come?'

'I don't know!' I blurt out. 'It's the truth!'

'You not know truth. Every day lie!' He slaps me again and I shriek. Mr Lee remains silent this time.

Sensing that he's getting nowhere and perhaps reminding himself of my value to him, Mr Choi decides to change tack and walks over to where Mr Lee has sunk himself onto the other chair and starts conversing with him. I glance around the room and shudder at the sight of Francesca's dried blood splattered all over the floor. My stomach tightens and I have to fight off the urge to throw up.

The two men talk for a long time, sometimes in heated tones, giving me the notion that they have no idea what to do next. Eventually, however, Mr Lee gets the brown envelope out of his pocket and hands it over to my captor, who immediately puts the gun down on a small table beside them and starts counting. After he has finished, he shows his feelings by shouting at Mr Lee for quite some time. Mr Lee points mutely at the wad of notes so Mr Choi counts it again. He reaches the end and the situation doesn't appear to have changed as he starts ranting away at Mr Lee once more, quite clearly outraged about something. I can only glean from the altercation that perhaps Mr Choi was expecting more money up front.

Mr Lee leans forward, as though exhausted by the whole thing, and then, while Mr Choi is waving the money around in a new fit of rage, swiftly grabs the gun from the table. He points it at Mr Choi and without a moment's hesitation shoots him twice.

He slumps down against the wall, looking startled, a shower of notes fluttering around him. He goes very still.

Mr Lee puts the gun back down on the table and looks at it for some time in apparent disbelief. Then he hangs his head in shame as though he cannot believe what has just happened. Neither can I.

'Mr Lee, are you okay?' I whisper.

There's no response. I wait for a moment. 'Min-Jun?'

He finally comes to and lifts his head to look at me.

'What happen me, Charlotte? My life ruin. I go prison for this.' He starts to cry.

I'm conscious of the fact that I'm still tied to a chair in a tiny room with a man, who is both very upset and in possession of a gun.

'Mr Choi,' I tell him soothingly, 'was a bad man. A very bad man. You can see that. I know it's hard for you right now but you did the right thing.'

He stares at me. Then he gets up slowly from his chair. My heart lurches as he picks the gun up from the table and comes towards me.

'Really?' he says. 'You think so? I not know any more. My childrens... They think I good man. Look what happen.' He kneels down before me and sobs bitterly into my lap.

'I'm sure everything can get better for you now,' I try to reassure him. 'Me and you… we can be together. Yes, I'm sure of it.'

He looks up at me but does not say anything.

'But we need to get rid of his body,' I continue. 'Maybe there's a lake or something close by. We could throw the body and the gun in the lake. Then we could go away somewhere together. Far away from here –

176

somewhere we could be safe. Just imagine it. You and I together…'

Still knelt down in front of me, he puts the barrel of the gun in his mouth and places his finger on the trigger, apparently unresponsive to everything I've just said.

'Min-Jun, no!' I beg. 'Please don't do this! You're scaring me! I've seen enough bloodshed and I don't want to be all alone here. What about our future together? Please listen to me!'

Sweat is pouring down his face as he contemplates ending it all right now, rolling the gun around in his mouth.

'Min-Jun, I love you,' I burst out. 'Please don't do this. We have a future together! Take the gun out of your mouth. I'm begging you!'

He looks up at me and gazes into my eyes. Finally, after what feels like an eternity, he takes the gun out of his mouth.

'It too late, Charlotte. They find us,' he whispers through his tears.

'It's not too late. I have a plan. Please listen to me, would you?'

I tell him my plan again but this time he's paying attention, taking everything in. He mulls the idea over.

'Yes… maybe good idea,' he replies at last, a small smile returning to his face.

I smile back at him.

Gotcha!

'Why don't you untie me so we can get the body in the car?'

He gets up and puts the gun in his jacket pocket before kissing me on my cheek and going over to Mr Choi's dead body to search through his pockets for the key to the handcuffs. Having found it, he comes back and unties my hands and unlocks the cuffs.

Once free I give him a hug.

One down, one to go!

177

'We need to be quick,' I warn him.

'Yes, you right. We need bag for body.'

He searches around for a while and finally finds something suitable. He carries a large rug over to where Mr Choi's body is slumped.

'Okay. Roll his body in the rug – and make sure you get his car keys,' I instruct him.

He takes off his jacket and places it on the back of one of the chairs, then sets about covering the body, after first retrieving the car keys. He mutters away to himself as things start to get messy, but eventually the job is done.

He sits down, looking shattered from the turn of events. He has blood smeared on his face and there are big red splashes all over his white shirt.

'You need to clean yourself up, Min-Jun.'

He looks down at his bloodstained shirt and agrees.

'Maybe there are some clothes that you can change into somewhere else around here,' I suggest. 'Let's go and look.'

He gets up and is just about to leave the room when he turns back and picks his jacket up from the back of the chair.

Chance gone!

We pad upstairs into the silent house, which looks just as run down as the hostess bar. We soon find a bedroom and I scan the room, looking for a wardrobe with shirts in it. My attention is drawn to a Russian doll that is placed on the window sill. It looks strangely out of place among the other oriental ornaments. I walk towards the wardrobe and select a clean white shirt on a hanger.

'Is this okay for you?'

'Yes. Now you come with me. Bring shirt,' he orders.

He leads the way towards the adjoining bathroom.

I follow reluctantly.

I'm not a free woman quite yet.

178

Chapter Twenty-five

Having cleaned himself up in the bathroom Mr Lee puts on the shirt and his jacket and smoothes his hair in the mirror. Then he gets out his mobile phone and starts tapping away.

'What are you doing?' I enquire suspiciously.

'I go on net. Find lake.'

I breathe a silent sigh of relief. 'Yes, that's a good idea.'

He spends a couple of minutes on his phone, then puts it away in his jacket pocket.

'There's lake near here. I think we take body there,' he tells me.

'Great! How far away is it?'

'Very close.'

'It needs to be a deep lake, though. We never want it to be discovered,' I warn him.

'Oh, yes, this lake one of deepest Korea. They never find body.'

I smile inwardly as I can see my plan is coming to fruition.

'Well, we'd better get this finished with then,' I say brightly.

He surprises me by cupping my face in his hands and gazing lovingly into my eyes. As much as I hate it, I play along with it.

'I feel better now you here,' he murmurs.

He moves his hand onto my breast and starts massaging it. He attempts to kiss me but I pull my head back gently, trying not to let him realise that I'm squirming inside at him touching me.

'Let's get rid of the body first and then we'll have plenty of opportunities later on,' I whisper playfully into his ear.

I sense that he's aroused by my presence but his expression becomes serious again as I remind him of the dead body in the room below. When he speaks again his voice is heavy with resignation.

'Okay, but later special night.'

'I look forward to it,' I reply, brushing his cheek with my lips.

You ain't having any more 'special nights' with me, sicko!

He takes me by the waist and leads me back down to the other room. We enter the room and approach the wrapped-up body.

He bends down and starts gathering up his money and putting it back in the envelope, but leaving the notes that are heavily stained in Mr Choi's blood. Once finished he puts the envelope back in his jacket pocket and tells me to take the corpse's legs while he lifts the upper part of the body. We drag our burden out of the room and back down the corridor towards the garage.

'Are you okay?' asks Mr Lee when I have to pause for breath.

'Yes, I just need to catch my breath for a moment,' I gasp as I lean against the wall.

He lays the bag on the floor and lights a cigarette for himself, then takes a long puff. A morose look appears on his face.

'I never think this happen in my life. Before I happy. Happy marriage, two baby. So happy. But my job. They make me work long hour so I see family not so much. Everyone in Korea work too much hour. My wife, I not know her now. I no remember why we love each other.'

He puts the cigarette to his mouth again and takes in another hit.

'I'm sorry to hear that,' I respond. 'But there's one thing I don't understand. Why come to see me when you could be with your family in the evenings?'

180

'Ah, I explain you. Korea it important to socialise after work. So much time we go for dinner and drink. Much worker don't have family meal so we think stay out.'

'Why not go home after the meal?'

'It difficult. When boss go home we go home, but no before. It Korean culture. No see childrens, and wife sleeping when worker go home.'

I actually start to feel a twinge of sympathy for him, but then I recall the night he raped me and all I can think of is destroying this sorry excuse for a man.

'I'm so sorry to hear that,' I reply.

He drops his cigarette and stubs it out with his shoe. 'We must continue.' He sounds weary and fed up with it all.

'Try to think of the future and us,' I repeat, not wanting him to throw in the towel just yet.

We manage to drag the body back to the car, where we heave it into the boot like it's a sack of spuds. He shuts the boot firmly and we get into the front seats. He puts the key in the ignition and starts the engine.

'Do you know the way?' I ask.

'Car has sat nav. Everything okay,' he answers.

We set off but hit a problem when we reach the gates. He looks perplexed as he tries to fathom out how to open them. I recall Mr Choi opening them with a button inside the car so we search around and finally locate it. The gates slowly open to let us out.

It's still pitch black as we drive out onto the bumpy single-track road. I check the time. It's twelve thirty-five. He crunches the gears as he builds up speed. He laughs it off, saying that he needs time to get used to the car. I grip my seat as he goes faster still and try to figure out what happens next…

'Are we near the lake yet?'

Mr Lee takes a hand off the wheel and consults his phone. The car reverberates as we hit a bump in the road.

'Please be careful,' I tell him.

'No worry. I very good driver. I look after you,' he assures me. 'We there soon. Fifteen minutes.'

I take a quick look at the time on the dashboard. It's twelve fifty-one.

He sighs. He sounds like he is becoming depressed again.

'I no believe this happen...'

'We'll soon be rid of him and can get away from here. Where do you want to live?' I say in a deliberately upbeat voice.

He glances at me and places his hand on my thigh.

I grit my teeth and let his hand stay there.

'You know you only reason why I still here,' he remarks, stating the obvious. 'Yes, you right. We lose him and drive safe place. I have apartment far from Seoul. We go there together. Maybe leave Korea. I have family North Korea.'

Hearing those two words makes me shudder. I recall what my mother said when she was scolding me just before I left the country. *All those nuclear missiles sent flying around by Kim Jong what's-his-face's regime in North Korea...* My heart sinks.

We come to a big road sign that looks familiar to me. I look for the word 'Danger' – and sure enough it's there. At least we're going the right way.

'This road is dangerous. Be careful,' I say as he steers the car off the road.

He takes his hand off my thigh and abruptly stops the car. I freeze. He switches on the door light and I can see that his face has turned an angry shade of red.

'How you know?' he demands.

Fearing I have given the game away, I think quickly. 'The road sign. It said "danger", so that's how I know.'

He stares at me for several seconds, weighing up what I've told him. His face is still red with rage. He turns off the light and we carry on waiting there in the dark, which only intensifies my fear. I feel my palms go sweaty so clench my fists, worried that he might try to hold my hand. Finally, however, he starts the car and puts it into reverse. I wipe my hand dry on my skirt. He stops at the sign and reads it.

'Ah, I see,' he murmurs. 'Sign in English.'

He plants his hand on my thigh again and I place my own on top of it.

'Let's just get rid of the body and get out of here,' I urge him. 'It gives me the creeps. Please drive carefully, though.'

He sets off again down the bumpy track at a sensibly low speed.

Having coped with the drop in elevation that nearly caught Mr Choi out last time, we arrive at the lake and he stops the car. Before he jumps out he checks the map of the lake on his phone. He then opens his door and comes around to my side of the vehicle.

'Quick. We must put body in lake then go.'

I get out and he links arms with me, perhaps making sure that I cannot escape, and we go to the boot of the car. I look around in the hope that Seoyeon has revealed everything to the police and that they are here waiting to pounce, but my mood darkens as I see nothing unusual.

Don't let it get to you.

He opens the boot and sets about getting the body out. While he's struggling with it, I contemplate slamming the boot on him but at that moment he looks around at me and foils my plan. Once the body is out and it's lying on the floor, he tells me to pick it up and drag it the remaining distance to the lake. Meanwhile he takes out the gun and holds it in his hand as he checks that we are unobserved.

183

I summon all of my energy to drag the body to the lake. He uses the light on his phone to show me the way. We follow the same overgrown path I went down with Mr Choi until we approach the large open overhang. I look to my left and spot the ornate building once again dimly lit up against the night sky. I let the body drop on the ground and take in some deep breaths.

He looks at the map on his phone again. 'Okay, we go right. This is quick way.' Then he goes still as his attention is drawn to something else. 'What that noise?'

'I can't hear anything.'

'Quiet! Listen,' he says softly.

It becomes apparent to me now as I hear the familiar throbbing noise of a helicopter. I look up and see a searchlight scanning an area over in the distance to our right. He looks up and sees it too.

I grab hold of him as he appears to freeze, rooted to the spot.

'We have to get rid of this body now! Then we need to get out of here. We can do this together,' I tell him calmly.

He starts speaking to himself in Korean, leaving me unsure as to his exact thoughts.

'We have no time for this, Min-Jun. I want to be with you, so we need to act now before they find us!'

Without warning he lifts the gun and holds it against my head.

'You do this to me!' he hisses.

I can feel the gun pressing against my temple. 'No, I didn't! You have to believe me! I love you, Min-Jun. I want to be with you.'

He speaks in Korean again, shouting loudly to himself.

'Min-Jun, we have to act now!'

I try to shake him out of it, ignoring the gun he's pointing at me. The noise of the helicopter gets ever louder as the searchlight shines on the glimmering surface of the lake.

'I not know you any more!' he yells. 'You lie!'

'I'm here now with a gun to my head and I'm telling you that I love you! You have to believe me!' I move towards him and kiss him on the lips.

Stale cigarettes! Suck it up.

He suddenly springs into action and hurries to the body lying on the ground.

'We go now!'

We grab an end each and race along the overgrown path at breakneck speed. I stumble, dropping the body on the floor. The rug unravels, exposing the dead body.

'No time! We must go!' he screams as I double up in pain and gasp for breath.

The sound of the helicopter grows louder as it gets ever nearer. I straighten up and can see the searchlight shining towards the ornate building. I drag the body towards the edge of the overhang. He looks over the edge of the drop and then signals at me to roll the body over it.

'Push now!' he demands, as the searchlight starts moving in our direction.

'We need something to weigh the body down. You're not thinking clearly!' I shout.

'You blind? No see light, hear noise? No time!' I hear the click of his gun. 'Do it now!'

'The body will be found if we don't weight it down. Is that what you want? I want us to be together!' I scream, trying to make him see sense.

I look up and see that the searchlight is directly above me. I transfer my gaze towards him and see desperation in his eyes. A frightened little boy stands in front of me, welling up inside.

'I love you, Charlotte,' he says quietly.

I'm distracted by an amplified voice from a megaphone in the helicopter and raise my eyes once more, squinting in the beam of the searchlight. When I look away again for him, he's nowhere to be seen. All I can see is a tangle of bushes invading a desolate pathway.

Realising that I'm all alone, I wave my hands frantically in the air and shout for help with all of the strength left in me.

'Please don't move! Step away from the body,' orders the voice from the helicopter.

I wait there in fear for several minutes until I hear police sirens in the near distance. Minutes later I'm surrounded by police officers all pointing their guns at me. My heart races as I raise my trembling hands in surrender.

Part Three
Chapter Twenty-six

'Please take a seat,' says a smartly dressed police officer. He hands me a cup of coffee and sits down next to me. 'The detective will be with you soon,' he adds.

I wait in the interrogation room with him for a few minutes until the door opens and a familiar figure walks in, shutting the door behind him. He steps towards the other side of the desk and sits down opposite me.

'Hello,' he greets me. 'I'm Senior Inspector Sang. We met at the hostess bar earlier this evening. I think I told you that I speak English fluently so don't worry about the language barrier.'

'Hello, Senior Inspector.'

I notice that he's still dressed in the same dark suit that he was wearing at the club. The other police officer gets up from his seat, bows to the inspector and leaves the room. The inspector reaches into the top drawer and pulls out a notepad and a Dictaphone.

'I know you've been through an ordeal but we need to spend some time with you to ascertain exactly what has happened,' he tells me gently. 'Firstly, I need to take down your details.'

We spend several minutes going through my personal details as he scribbles the information down. Then he sets up the Dictaphone.

'Interview commences at three thirty-four a.m. So, tell me exactly what happened. Just take your time,' he instructs me.

My stomach churns as I realise I'm going to have to relive everything I've gone through to a near total stranger. I feel my hands tremble as I begin telling him my story, about how I was kidnapped and ended up being forced to work in the hostess club.

He makes notes as I go along, then starts to ask questions as he reads back through them.

'As I understand it so far, you were abducted by Mr Yi and he shot Chris dead in the car while you were being driven from the airport to your language school in Seoul. You don't know Chris's surname but you say that he worked somewhere in Seoul and that his body was dumped in the lake near Sinsan-Ri.'

'That's right, but I do know the name of his colleague in London,' I inform him. 'He is Colin Bliss, who works at a recruitment agency. He'll know Chris's full name.'

'So what's the name of this business and how does it operate?'

'Colin's the owner of SK Recruitment agency and he interviewed me in London. He said that Chris would meet me at the airport upon my arrival. He also told me that Chris worked in Seoul and looked after the business over here. He came with Mr Yi that day, calling him a new driver and introducing him as "Mr Kim".'

'Ah, Mr Kim is a very common surname in this country. Maybe he was trying to cover his tracks.'

The inspector's tight-lipped expression makes me feel that he's heard this trick played many times before. He politely asks me to continue.

'I lost consciousness while Mr Yi was pointing a gun at Chris. The next thing I knew I was bound and gagged in a room above the club.' I feel my hands beginning to shake.

Nobody can get at you now. Just calm down!

The inspector looks puzzled. 'Hold on a minute. There's something I don't understand. Where exactly were you when you lost consciousness?'

'We were on our way to Seoul from the airport. Mr Yi drove down a quiet road and pulled a gun on Chris. I don't know where exactly but it must have been close to the airport because we'd only been driving for a short time.'

The inspector frowns at me. 'And for what reason did you lose consciousness?'

'Mr Yi gave me a bottle of water when I got in the car and being very thirsty I drank it in one go. I think there was something in it because I felt incredibly sleepy soon afterwards.'

'It could have been because of the long journey from the UK, couldn't it?'

I shake my head. 'I don't think so. The water left a funny aftertaste in my mouth. I'm sure he drugged me. In fact, I'm absolutely positive!' I feel the anger bubbling up inside me as the memories come flooding back.

Keep calm!

The inspector makes some more notes before continuing. 'Just try to keep a clear mind. I'm only trying to get a good picture of everything, that's all. Anything you can tell me will be most beneficial. Mr Yi's here in police custody so we can question him later.'

'This whole thing was obviously planned in advance,' I tell him. 'I would like to know how Mr Yi knew I was coming on that day and who was involved in my abduction.'

'As I said before, we'll question Mr Yi in the coming days to try to get to the bottom of this. Do you think Mr Bliss has anything to do with your abduction?'

'I have no idea…' I pause. 'Mr Yi was described as a fairly new driver and I don't know who interviewed him for the job. Presumably it was Chris in Seoul.' I look hard at him. 'Do you have anyone else in custody?'

'There are certain individuals we intend to talk to in order to establish what has happened here,' he replies vaguely.

189

I begin to feel impatient with him for not divulging the suspects' names.

'Did you catch Mr Lee?' I ask, in the hope that he might at least tell me that.

'Yes, a man by the name of Mr Lee is with us in police custody.'

My irritation with the inspector subsides as it slowly sinks in that the horrible excuse for a man didn't get away.

'So, can you tell me how Mr Lee's involved in all this?' the inspector enquires.

'He was a regular client at the bar and always chose to be with me because he saw me as something a bit different. He liked to practise his limited English on me.' I take a gulp of coffee and see that my hand is trembling violently. I push the cup away.

The inspector notices. 'I can tell that this is painful for you to talk about, but you must tell me everything that you know,' he says softly.

I put the cup down on the table and nod my head in compliance. 'At first it was just chatting and singing songs to him. He liked my voice and loved it when I sang the Beatles to him. But the more he came, the more he wanted me.' A lump forms in my throat and I'm finding it increasingly difficult to talk about him.

'Would you like some water, Charlotte?' he asks.

I nod my head so he walks over to the water cooler and pours some into a glass, handing it over to me. I sip it gratefully.

'He kept putting his hand on my thigh and rubbing it up and down, patting it,' I tell him in a taut voice. 'It was disgusting. I hated it. But I felt as though Mr Choi was always keeping tabs on me, so I let it happen more often. If I didn't then...' I stop to take another sip.

'If you want these people to be brought to justice you must tell us everything,' the inspector says firmly.

190

'If I didn't do what he said he would get angry with me. I had no choice!' I attempt to put the glass back on the table but my hand is shaking so much I misjudge it and it smashes on the floor. I apologise and bend down to start picking up the pieces but he tells me not to worry about it.

'Take your time. Just try to relax. I'm not one of those bad guys.'

'Mr Lee raped me!' I suddenly blurt out. 'He paid money to Mr Choi, took me into one of the rooms at the back and raped me.'

After keeping it all pent up inside me for so long, I feel shattered now I've said it and rest my head on the table, trying not to hyperventilate. I hear the inspector's voice talking to me but it sounds a long way away, as though everything he says is being sucked into the air that surrounds me. Eventually, though, his words become clearer.

'These are strong allegations you are making, Charlotte, but I think you need time to recover. I think we should take a fifteen-minute break.' He bends over the Dictaphone. 'Interview suspended at three forty-eight a.m.'

Chapter Twenty-seven

'Are you ready to resume?' Inspector Sang asks as he sits down behind the desk with the Dictaphone in his hand.

I'm determined to see this through now. 'Yes, let's get this finished with,' I answer.

'Interview restarts at five past four a.m. So, you just told me that Mr Lee raped you. I know this is really hard, but you have to tell me exactly what happened.'

My hands start to tremble.

Get this over and done with and you will be on your way home. Mind over matter.

'Mr Lee paid Mr Choi to have sex with me on two separate occasions. The first time we went to one of the rooms behind the red curtains in the bar. He forced himself on me. I didn't want any of it but who could I turn to? I had nobody on my side.'

I drink some water. I'm trembling from head to toe.

'When did this happen?'

'I don't know. I have no concept of the dates. Every day was just the same!'

'It's vital that you tell us when it happened, if you can.' He checks his notes. 'Okay, so you said there were two occasions. Can you tell me what happened on the second occasion?'

I take a deep breath. 'The second time I made sure that I got him drunk as we sat together at the table, in the hope that he wouldn't be able to perform. By the time we got to the room he was very intoxicated. I poured out some more soju for him so that he was unable to get an erection and it worked. He ended up getting very abusive, taking a video of me performing sexual acts for him on his phone.' I stop and wipe the tears away from my face.

'I have to know everything, Charlotte,' says the inspector in a serious tone of voice. 'Did anyone else try to rape you?'

'No, it was just him. Mr Choi said he preferred brunettes.' I rack my brains. 'He did try it on once with me but fortunately his phone rang. He seemed to lose interest in me again shortly after that.'

'How about Mr Yi?'

'No, he never tried to rape me.' I remember the mobile phone. 'Mr Lee's phone is hidden in the apartment above the club. Have you found it yet?'

'Not yet, I'm afraid. We are still searching the bar and apartment. Ms Park – maybe you know her as Seoyeon – informed us about it being there but you didn't tell her where it was located. Can you tell me now so I can contact one of the officers?'

I knew she would come good.

'So was she your tip-off?'

He nods his head and my thoughts turn back to the hidden mobile.

'The phone is in the bathroom of the apartment, where I was being held. I wanted to keep it in a safe place so I hid it behind the toilet.'

'Thank you. I'll pass the information on. That'll be needed for evidence. So how did you manage to acquire Mr Lee's phone?'

'As I said, I got him drunk and he put the phone on the table after filming me but forgot about it so I picked it up when he wasn't looking. It's a small phone so I was able to hide it when I was led back upstairs to the apartment by Mr Choi. If you find that phone, you'll see what kind of man he is. How did you catch him?'

'He got in the car and sped off down a dangerous single-track road. Half way down the track he veered to the left to avoid a collision with an oncoming police car. He ended up putting the car in the ditch, puncturing a tyre in the process. With nowhere to run, he gave

193

himself up and handed over the weapon he was carrying.'

I manage a wry smile. 'I'm happy that he's been caught. He deserves everything he gets!'

Scumbag!

'There's one thing I don't understand, Charlotte. You said you didn't have any friends, but Seoyeon seems to have helped you a lot. Can you please explain?'

'What I meant was that I didn't have any friends at that time. Seoyeon replaced a girl from the Philippines…' I start to cry.

'Take your time.' Inspector Sang hands me a box of tissues so I wipe my face and blow my nose. 'What happened to the girl from the Philippines?'

'Her name was Francesca. She helped me to escape but Mr Choi caught us both outside and took us to his house near the lake and killed her there right in front of me. Then he made me drop her body in the lake.' I start crying again as I think about that dreadful night.

'I know this is difficult and I'm almost finished, but I have to ask you about Seoyeon. You said you had no friends but now you tell me about Francesca and Seoyeon. Just tell me everything you know about them, please.'

One last push.

'Francesca didn't want to get involved at first but she knew that what was happening there wasn't right. I was desperate and she was the only one who could speak enough English to help me out. What she did for me was truly heroic and I'll never forget her.'

'So what happened after Francesca died?'

'At that point I had almost no hope left,' I whisper. 'I considered ending my own life. The one thing that kept me going was the thought of Mr Lee's mobile phone that was hidden in the bathroom. I thought that I might be able to use it to contact my parents but just as I was tapping in the number the battery died.'

194

'Oh, dear. That was unfortunate. But you spoke to your mother in the end, didn't you?'

'She contacted you then?' I ask. The thought of my parents coming to my aid brightens my mood a little.

'She contacted the British Embassy,' he confirms.

'That's wonderful…' I momentarily lose my track of thought as images of my parents fill my mind.

'Charlotte? Is everything okay?'

'Sorry. I was just thinking about my parents.' I get back to the story. 'I managed to get into Mr Choi's office and spoke briefly to my mother but someone walked in so I put the phone down and hid under the desk.'

'Someone?'

'It was the hostess manager, Mi-Young. She was very close to Mr Choi. She must have known what was going on.'

'Why do you think that?'

'Like I said, the three of them were very close. Mi-Young, Mr Yi and Mr Choi were as thick as thieves at times. It's just a hunch, that's all.'

The inspector jots down some more notes.

'And how does Seoyeon fit into all of this?' he enquires, looking up at me.

'She replaced Francesca after she was killed. I had a feeling that Mr Choi didn't want to employ anyone from anywhere other than South Korea so as to stop me talking to people about my predicament. But what he didn't know was that she was highly educated and could speak English.' I take a sip of water. 'She had read about my disappearance on the BBC website and was convinced it was me. When she confronted me I told her not to get involved, but it was to no avail.'

He scribbles down some more information. 'So we move on to my final question. Can you tell me what happened after I was asked to move to another table last night?'

195

I pause to collect my thoughts. 'After you left me I was asked to go to Mr Choi's office. Mr Lee was also present and they were in deep conversation. There was an envelope on the table but it wasn't until we got in the car that I found out what it was all about.' A thought suddenly springs to mind which I think is worth exploring further. 'I remember Mr Choi telling me that the apartment block was all his. He told me his plans for the place but I had the impression that he didn't have enough money to renovate it. That's why he wanted me at his bar, because I was something different and it appealed to some of the richer clients. I don't know that much about it but perhaps abducting me was a cheaper alternative to hiring Russian girls,' I add.

'Okay. Now tell me more about the envelope. I assume there was money in it.'

'When we got in the car Mr Lee told me that he wanted to buy me. He was obsessed with me by now and couldn't seem to get enough.' I shudder again. 'I hate him so much!'

'Take your time.'

'We got back to the house and Mr Choi handcuffed me and then tied me to a chair. Mr Lee just sat there and watched it happen. The envelope came out and Mr Choi started counting the money but once he had finished he became angry, shouting at Mr Lee. He started waving the money around in the air, so Mr Lee picked the gun up and shot him twice.' The lump has come back into my throat so I gulp down some more water.

The inspector has his pen poised. 'So what happened next?'

'Mr Lee looked like he couldn't believe his own actions. He talked about his family and mentioned his children. He wanted to end his own life, putting the gun in his mouth, but I dissuaded him from doing that by convincing him that we still had a future together.'

The inspector looks pensively at me. 'Why did you say that?'

'I was in the middle of nowhere and the only person who could help me was him! I had told Seoyeon about the lake while I was with her in the bathroom at the club so I thought that if I could get Mr Lee to drive me to the lake, the police might just turn up and rescue me.'

'And so it proved.' The inspector sits back in his chair, suggesting that he's almost done. 'Is there anything else that you want to tell me?'

'I can't think of anything right now, but I'll have a think tonight and if I've missed anything, I'll let you know.'

'Okay, I will bear everything you have told me in mind. I want to keep you in the picture. We will need to interview everyone involved so it will take some time for us to collate all the information. I'll be in contact with you again soon.'

The inspector closes his notepad.

'If you find any of my personal belongings, will I get them back?' I ask.

'Yes, you'll get those back at some point.' He gets up from his chair and comes around to my side of the table to switch off the Dictaphone. 'Meanwhile, your father is waiting outside for you.'

I feel my mouth drop open in surprise. 'My dad is here?'

He nods his head. I rise and thank him, unable to suppress the huge smile that spreads across my face as I hurry to the door.

A police officer shows me to the waiting room. He opens the door and my heart leaps for joy.

'Charlotte!' My dad erupts from his seat and rushes towards me. He stops in front of me with his arms held wide. 'What has happened to you, my darling? Come here, my poor child.'

We share a warm embrace and then both break down in floods of tears. I am reminded of the countless hugs he gave me when I was a young child growing up in the safety of two loving parents, who were always doing their best for me.

Eventually I stop crying and get my breath back. 'Dad, I just want to get out of here, right now. My mind is all mushy. I just need some rest,' I mumble semi-coherently.

'I'll take you back to my hotel and get you a room next to mine. I flew here as soon as we realised there was something wrong. We've got a lot to catch up on, but all in good time. I've contacted your mum at home and she's over the moon to hear you're safe. I'm just so happy to see you!'

After a word or two with the officers present, we leave the police station just before sunrise and take a taxi back to my dad's hotel. Upon our arrival he books a room for me next to his one.

'Okay, this is my room,' he tells me, 'and I believe the next one is yours. Take your time, love. Just get plenty of rest.'

As I stand there ready to go to my room I suddenly freeze as my emotions build up inside me, overwhelming me with shame.

'Dad?'

'Yes, love?'

'I'm so sorry for being such a disappointment to you both.' I burst out crying.

'Never say that! You're not a disappointment,' he says firmly.

'I am to mum! If only you knew what they did to me…' I slump to the floor.

He gets on his knees and embraces me.

'Your mum has been out of her mind with worry and just wants her daughter back.'

198

He picks me up and opens the door to my room. We embrace each other again and then he leaves me to rest. I close the door and lock it. Tired and exhausted, I plonk myself down on the bed, wipe away my tears and sink into profound sleep.

Chapter Twenty-eight

I'm awoken by a knock on my door so I get up blearily and open it. Dad asks me if I would like to go downstairs and have some breakfast in the hotel restaurant. I quickly get ready and meet him there.

'Here you are.' He hands me a tray with a cup of coffee and some cereal on it. 'How did you sleep?'

'Well, the bed was certainly more comfortable than I've been used to – but I feel like I was only asleep for five minutes,' I respond wearily.

'You must call your mum later. She'll be dying to hear your voice.'

'Yes, okay.'

I add a drop of milk to my coffee.

He shakes his head. 'Charlotte, I can't believe what's happened to you. You read about these things in the papers but never expect it to be your own flesh and blood…' His voice trails off.

'I thought I'd never see you again,' I tell him, trying not to cry.

'We did our best to find you. That Mr Bliss wasn't very helpful at all.'

'Why? What happened?'

'Well, when we hadn't heard from you after a day or two we decided to contact him, but I couldn't find his details.'

'But I remember you writing the information down.'

'Yes, but the notepad wasn't there so I wrote it on the back of an envelope. I must have put it somewhere but I just couldn't remember where.' He looks apologetically at me.

'Oh, I see. And mum has the cheek to say that I'm the absent-minded one.'

'Well, anyway, I eventually found it a few days later in the back pocket of my jeans, which I don't wear that often – so I contacted him straightaway because we still hadn't heard anything from you. All he said was that it was "nothing out of the ordinary".'

'Oh, come on, dad! You know that I would have contacted you as soon as I could!' I can't keep the anger out of my voice.

'If you just let me finish, I'll tell you what I said to him.'

I agree to shut up.

'The man was impossible from the very beginning. He said that he wasn't responsible for you any more and it was clearly written down in your contract. So I asked him if he could contact the man you were meeting at the airport, but he said that they usually caught up with each other only once a fortnight and that he was unwilling to do so before then. He said he had a mountain of paperwork to get through, as if that was more important than my missing daughter. I found him to be extremely uncooperative!' He glares angrily at the tablecloth. 'After you called mum, I got the next flight here.' He places his hand on mine. 'I thought you said that a friend of yours had looked over the contract with a fine tooth comb?'

'I'm sorry, dad. I told a little white lie,' I tell him sheepishly.

He gives me an impatient look and removes his hand. 'A little white lie! Why on earth didn't you read the thing properly?'

'Every time I was going to look at it something cropped up!' I look at him in desperation. 'Please can we keep this between us? I don't want mum to know.'

He sighs. 'Okay, but you should know that it was very irresponsible – and look where it has got you.'

'I know, dad. I've learnt from my mistakes and I don't need any preaching from anyone. I've already paid the price. I've been in hell for the last couple of weeks, or however long it's been.'

He looks suddenly morose and I sense the guilt he's feeling.

'I'm sorry, darling. I've been so worried about you. The inspector said I should be prepared for the worst…' He breaks off, looking like a broken man.

My anger subsides and I begin to feel sorry for him as I realise the amount of pressure that he and my mother have been under.

'I don't want to rake over all of it again,' I tell him. 'I want to forget about it and move on.'

He nods his head in understanding.

I change the topic quickly. 'How's Rachel? Has she been in touch?'

'She's been really supportive. She visited us as soon as the story went public and even cooked us dinner. It was great to have her around because she kept our spirits up. She's a real good egg, that one.'

I smile. 'I can't wait to see her. I've really missed her. The only thing that I was allowed to keep was a picture of her and me. It kept me going when things got really bad.'

'You'll see her very soon, darling.'

The thought of finally going back home and seeing everyone again makes me feel better than I have done for ages.

'A smile!' he says, smiling himself. 'So nice to see.'

I knock back the rest of my coffee. 'Right, I think I'm going back to my room for another nap.'

'That's a good idea. You do look tired. Don't you worry about anything, love. I'm here for you now.'

After a couple of days of solid rest and without venturing outside the hotel, I receive a call to go back to the police station. My dad comes along with me and waits outside in the waiting room while I'm shown to the inspector's office.

'Hello, Charlotte,' says Inspector Sang. 'Please take a seat.'

I sit down opposite him and he opens a folder that's lying on the table between us. His pursed lips give nothing away and I begin to feel nervous.

He looks up at last. 'There's no need to look so worried. You aren't on trial here, Charlotte.' He smiles and that makes me feel a little better.

'We've now spoken to everyone who's involved in the case and also to the key witnesses. I've also managed to contact Mr Bliss and, after some initial resistance, he's agreed to cooperate fully with the investigation,' he tells me.

'So why did he refuse to cooperate in the first place?'

'He said that he was innocent and he didn't want to have anything to do with the case that might put his company's reputation in jeopardy. However, when we told him your account of what had happened to Chris and the fact that the press have picked up on the story, he changed his mind and wanted to clear his name.'

I'm impressed with how quickly the investigation has progressed. 'That's good news. Has anyone confirmed my testimony?'

The inspector pulls a face. 'It appears as though everything happened behind closed doors and the only person who's confirmed your testimony is Seoyeon, and she knows everything from you. The other witnesses never noticed anything because you never complained to them.'

'Oh,' I say, feeling deflated. 'So what did she say?'

'Once again, Seoyeon confirmed what you said, but the problem is she can only tell us what you told her. For this reason she's an unreliable witness.'

I don't like the negative sound of what he's saying. 'How about Mr Yi? What did he say?'

'He was a tough nut to crack but we dug up some information about him and used it against him so that he would talk.'

'So can you tell me what he said?'

'To cut a long story short, Mr Choi was in a lot of debt so he wanted to increase the number of clients at his hostess bar. He realised that he couldn't afford to employ Russian girls so it appears he targeted a recruitment agency in order to get a white foreign girl to work at his club. Mr Yi was ordered by Mr Choi to find work at a recruitment agency. They concocted a plan where Mr Yi was the driver, giving him an opportunity to kidnap a white girl. Unfortunately, that girl was you.'

'Oh, yes, it's all making sense to me now.' I say solemnly. 'I remember the time he took some money from the till.' My hands begin to tremble. 'And what did Mi-Young say?'

'She's refusing to cooperate so far, but we'll keep working on it.'

'So what's going to happen next?' I ask.

He holds his hands up. 'Unless you testify in court yourself we can't take it any further because we don't have enough proof.'

'Did you find the mobile phone I told you about?' I ask, clinging to the hope that this might be a key piece of evidence.

'Yes, we did, but again without your testimony any good judge will dismiss this as insufficient.'

I stare at him. 'You're not saying that I'll have to testify in front of everyone, are you?'

'I'm afraid there's no other way,' he says with authority.

'You can't do this to me! I can't go through all of this yet again!'

'At the end of the day it's up to you,' the inspector informs me. 'If you decide not to testify, we will not be able to proceed with the rape charge. We can still charge

Mr Lee with murder, but I would add that your testimony in court would still be invaluable due to the two crimes being closely linked.'

I hesitate for a few seconds. 'I need to think about it,' I tell him at last.

'Yes, of course. Give it some thought and I will be in touch with you very soon to find out your decision. Is there anything else you would like to discuss?'

I think for a moment. 'Have you recovered any of the dead bodies?'

'Yes, we've found three bodies. We are currently conducting post-mortems in order to identify them.'

'Three bodies, you say? I can't believe it.'

I wonder if the other body is Tatiana.

'It's too early to divulge any more information but as soon as we know more, we'll keep you posted,' he promises me. 'Do you have any other questions?'

Still in a state of shock, I struggle to think of the questions that I had prepared for prior to the interview.

'Did you find any of my belongings?'

'Unfortunately we need to keep them as evidence for the trial – but we do have your passport and you are now free to leave the country.'

He opens the drawer and hands me an envelope. I find my passport inside and breathe a huge sigh of relief. I can finally see the light at the end of the tunnel.

'Is there anything else you particularly want back?' the inspector enquires.

'There's a picture of my friend and me…' Thinking about Rachel makes me want to return to the UK as quickly as possible. 'I would like it back if that's okay. It helped me get through my ordeal.'

'We can send that to you after the trial. I have your address details on my piece of paper,' he confirms.

I thank him and leave his office then walk to the waiting room to meet my dad.

'How did it go, darling?'

'Dad, I can't believe it. They found three bodies in the lake!'

'What? I don't understand.'

'It's a long story. I'll explain everything later.'

'How about everything else?'

'Not as well as I thought it would. They want me to testify in court.'

He looks concerned. 'Is there no other way?'

'No, there isn't. A part of me wants him to pay for what he has done but the thought of appearing in front of all those people to give my testimony is making me feel sick right now.'

'I don't want you to get worked up over this, darling. Do you have your passport back?'

I nod my head and show him.

'Great! We could be on the next plane back to the UK and you can forget all about it. But you should know that whatever you decide I will give you my full support. Why don't you just get some rest? Perhaps going back to England will be the right thing to do.'

We hug each other and decide to go for something to eat back in the safe surroundings of the hotel while I mull over my options.

Chapter Twenty-nine

Having bought the plane tickets two days earlier, dad and I arrive at the airport to board our plane. I look around me and see the same fast food chain restaurant from which I bought a hamburger and chips when I first arrived. The memories come flooding back.

'Are you okay, darling?'

He is looking at me with concern etched all over his face.

'Yes, let's just get out of here. This place gives me the creeps.' In my mind I am replaying the nightmare I had of being hounded by press at the airport. 'Do you think we'll have to dodge any news reporters?'

'Oh, I don't think so, love. I booked the tickets in secret. But…' He breaks off.

'But what?'

He faces me, putting his hands on both of my shoulders. I wait for him to speak.

'I'm with you now so you don't have to say a word to anyone, okay?' he reassures me.

'Okay.' I start to weep so he puts his arms around me and gives me a warm hug.

'It's okay, love. Nobody can get to you now because they have to get past me first and that isn't going to be possible. Now let's get you home.'

Once through customs we get on the plane back to the UK. As it takes off I think about my time in the country and the contrast it made with what I had expected. My heart suddenly feels heavy as I think of the pictures in the brochure of all the smiling children I had been expecting to teach. A single teardrop rolls down my cheek. With some difficulty I push the memories aside and try to get some sleep. It's no good, though, so my dad reaches into his bag.

'Take some of these, darling. They'll help you get some rest.' He hands me a bottle of pills.

'I'm not sure about this,' I say nervously, recalling the last time I took one of these, albeit unwittingly.

'Well, they're there if you need them.'

He places his arm around me and I find I don't need the sleeping pills any more.

'Charlotte, we make it! North Korea! We free!' says Mr Lee gleefully as we drive over the border to the other side.

'Free from whom?' I say in a panic, thinking about what my mum said to me about the country's regime.

'We meet family in secret and take us home.'

He leans over onto my side in the car and starts kissing my neck, while his hand slides up my skirt. My whole body tenses and I try to push his hand away but it's all in vain as he easily overpowers me.

'No, I don't want this!'

'Charlotte, Charlotte!'

I open my eyes in a state of confusion, shaken to the core. 'What's happening?' I mumble.

'You were starting to shout, love. Are you okay?' dad says, looking worried.

I look around. We're on the plane.

'Oh God! Was I?'

'Don't worry, it wasn't that loud,' he says, smiling and trying to calm my nerves. 'We had some turbulence and maybe that didn't help. Do you want to talk about it?'

'We're on a plane, dad! How can you possibly expect me to talk about my personal feelings here?'

'Sorry, it was a stupid question. But what I meant was it might be a good idea if you talked it all through with a professional when you get back, don't you think?'

I ponder his suggestion for a while. 'Yes, you're probably right,' I say at last. 'I'm sorry if I was abrupt but it was a really bad dream.'

'Well when you arrive back home you'll see your friends and family again and...' He stops himself mid-sentence.

'Dad, what is it?'

'It's nothing to worry about, but you do know that the press have got hold of your disappearance so there will probably be some paparazzi taking snaps of you upon our arrival.'

'But, dad, back at the airport you said everything would be okay – there wouldn't be any press. Why did you lie to me?' I feel dumbfounded that he could have tried to fool me over such a thing.

'I'm sorry, love, but how could I tell you that when you were feeling so scared. We've been lucky that we've avoided their attention so far but it's the reality of the situation, I'm afraid. I'm just trying to look out for you, that's all.'

My thoughts turn to our impending arrival at Heathrow airport and I feel the panic rising. 'I really don't want that kind of attention. Can't you try and tell them to leave me alone? All I want is my privacy.'

'As I said before, they'll have to get past me first. I'm not going to let them get to you, no matter how difficult it might be – but you can see why I had to tell you.'

I see his point. 'Well, I suppose it's better for me to be prepared.'

'Try not to worry about it too much. The papers will soon be forgotten about and in the bin the next day. Dinner's going to be served soon. Why don't you take those pills after you've eaten something?' he suggests.

Several hours later I'm awoken from a deep sleep by a message from the cabin crew over the speakers.

'We will shortly be arriving at London Heathrow airport. Please make sure you're sat back down in your seat and are wearing your seatbelt. Thank you for your cooperation.'

A few minutes later we are back on the ground and queuing to leave the aircraft. I smile as I look forward to seeing friends and family again, but then the possibility of being mobbed by the press makes my smile disappear as quickly as it arrived.

'Dad, do you think we could arrange to slip quietly out of the airport?' I whisper as we walk towards border control.

He thinks about my question. 'I don't think so, darling. I know it's going to be really tough for you but the media have been following this story closely and have been incredibly supportive on the whole.'

We go through customs and then collect our luggage from the conveyor belt.

'Okay now,' he says, looking at me. 'Just be prepared.'

I start to tremble as we approach the main exit doors.

'I don't think I can do this, dad,' I say nervously.

'It's all right, love.' He grabs my hand and leads the way.

The doors open and I'm greeted by a cacophony of sound from a throng of reporters and photographers. As my dad leads me onwards I begin to make out individual questions.

'How are you, Charlotte?' says one sympathetically.

'Welcome back, Charlotte,' says another.

'What's happened to the perpetrators? Are you going to testify? Did you do anything to lead them on?' demands a third.

I shrink against dad, who plants himself between me and the rank of reporters on the other side of the metal barrier.

'My daughter has no comment to give right now. Please respect that she's been through a traumatic experience.'

At the end of the line I finally see some familiar looking faces and my heart sings. My mum is first, rushing up to me and giving both of us a hug, followed by some other close family members.

'Charlotte, it's so good to see you!' cries mum with tears running down her cheeks.

'Mum!' It's all that I can muster as I'm hugged and kissed by my relatives. Then, just beyond them, I spot Rachel, who's standing back and waiting for her turn, smiling. After the group hug breaks up and the paparazzi have had their fill of pictures, I rush towards her.

'Rachel!'

'Hi, Char!'

'I've been waiting so long to be called that.'

'Come here, you.'

We embrace each other, both of us crying our eyes out.

'Once you're better you're coming over to mine and we'll have a nice glass of red and chat about normal things,' she manages to say between fits of uncontrollable weeping.

I get a flashback to my miserable little cell back in Seoul. 'That photo of us kept me going, you know. It was the only possession they let me keep!'

We collapse into each other's arms.

'Is this all over now?' she asks tentatively.

'The investigation is ongoing but I don't think I want to go back there ever again, Rach.'

'All that matters right now is that you're safe and back home with your family.'

When we have all recovered a little we head off towards the terminal exit. Rachel suddenly turns and taps me on the shoulder, then cups her hand over my ear.

'I can't believe it, Char,' she whispers, 'but twat-face is walking towards us. Do you want me or your dad to deal with him?'

I take a deep breath. 'No, Rach. I'm going to deal with this myself. It's the only way.'

Joe appears in front of me, holding a bunch of flowers.

'Oi!' dad growls. 'What the hell are you doing here? Clear off before–'

'Dad, calm down!' I interrupt. 'Leave this to me.'

Joe grins wolfishly. 'Babe, can I speak to you in private, just for a minute?'

'Okay – but just a minute.'

'Oh, what's she doing now?' I hear mum wail behind me, but I don't want to argue with her right now.

I walk Joe a few yards away from the others. 'Well?'

'These are for you,' he says, handing the bouquet to me.

I take it, then I glance over Joe's shoulder and register my mum's shocked expression.

'I can't believe this has happened to you, babe,' Joe continues nonchalantly. 'If you need any help whatsoever just ask. I've been so worried about you.'

I give him a long look. 'You know what makes me sick right now?'

He looks blankly at me.

'No?'

He remains expressionless.

'You really don't, do you?'

He frowns.

'You do! You're no better than those bastards I had to deal with out there. Take this as a word of warning. Don't ever come near me or text me again. Ever! Just fuck off, Joe!'

'But…' he stutters, looking confused.

'No buts. I suggest you turn around and leave quietly before I alert some of the journalists about how I got this scar.'

I begin to roll up my sleeve and that's enough to stop him in his tracks. Now he looks small and insignificant as the news slowly sinks into his tiny little brain. I turn my back on him and stride back towards my family with my head held high and a big smile on my face.

'Charlotte, why–'

I cut my mum off before her tongue dips into the acid.

'Before you go off on one, I won't be hearing from him *ever* again!'

My mum smiles. Maybe she sees that her naïve little girl has finally grown up. We head for the exit.

'Just wait a sec,' I tell everyone.

I rush over to a bin and stuff the flowers in it, then return to my parents.

'Everything okay, love?' asks dad.

'A fresh start away from him,' I say, feeling positive for the first time in ages.

I link arms with my parents and, followed by my friends, I emerge from the terminal deep in thought.

The End

I have also written a book, 'Kimchi with Everything: A Year in the Life of a TEFL Teacher', which gives a more uplifting account of my time teaching English in South Korea.

18721807R00120

Printed in Great Britain
by Amazon